STRANGE THINGS AND
STRANGER
†PLACES†

Tor books by Ramsey Campbell

Ancient Images
Cold Print
The Count of Eleven
Dark Companions
The Doll Who Ate His Mother
The Face That Must Die
Fine Frights (editor)
The Hungry Moon
Incarnate
The Influence
Midnight Sun
The Nameless
Obsession
The Parasite
Waking Nightmares

STRANGE THINGS AND
STRANGER
†PLACES†

RAMSEY CAMPBELL

TOR

A TOM DOHERTY ASSOCIATES BOOK

NEW YORK

STRANGE THINGS AND STRANGER PLACES

Copyright © 1993 by Ramsey Campbell

This book is printed on acid-free paper.

A Tor Book
Published by Tom Doherty Associates, Inc.
175 Fifth Avenue
New York, N.Y. 10010

Tor® is a registered trademark of Tom Doherty Associates, Inc.

Library of Congress Cataloging-in-Publication Data

Campbell, Ramsey.
      Strange things and stranger places / Ramsey Campbell.
          p.   cm.
      ISBN 0-312-85514-1
      I. Title.
      PR6053.A4855S75   1993
      823'.914—dc20   93-12758
                                                                       CIP

Book design by Lynn Newmark

First edition: June 1993

Printed in the United States of America

0 9 8 7 6 5 4 3 2 1

† COPYRIGHTS & ACKNOWLEDGMENTS †

for who else but Tom Doherty

† CONTENTS †

STRANGE THINGS AND
STRANGER
†PLACES†

† INTRODUCTION †

The strangest place most of us ordinarily see is the world, but familiarity tends to make us forget how strange it is. One thing good horror fiction—and, I'd suggest, any good fiction—can do is remind us. Of the stories in this book, "Needing Ghosts" certainly did that to me, and much else besides. If everything a writer creates is a stage in the process of getting to what he writes next, then perhaps I can claim that the rest of the contents lead to "Needing Ghosts."

Well, let me leave the exploration of that theme to anyone who finds it interesting. "Cat and Mouse" (1971) was the earliest tale I ever wrote to order, for the first anthology to be edited by a fantasy fan of about my own age with whom I'd corresponded while at school,

Michel Parry. The book was, I need hardly say, a collection of supernatural tales about cats. Reviewing it in *Fantastic,* Fritz Leiber criticised my story for coming on too feline too early. As usual in his criticisms, he was right, and his comment was the reason why I introduced the theme of "The Chimney" more gradually, but I don't think it's malicious of me to point out that the feline images in the opening sentences of "Cat and Mouse" were added at Michel's request. I hope they and my comments won't seem too intrusive.

Writing on a subject provided by an editor can be a useful discipline. "Cat and Mouse" now looks to me like one of my more controlled stories from the period after I'd completed *Demons by Daylight* and found myself writing in search of new themes. Some of the results of that process appear in *The Height of the Scream,* and some, to my relief, have never appeared anywhere. One such muffled story was "Property of the Ring," among the few tales I wrote in 1970. Dissatisfaction with it deterred me from even preparing a typescript, but I did feel the basic theme deserved another chance. When I began to write fulltime in 1973 and the horror markets immediately vanished like so many will-o'-the-wisps, I thought it might do as the basis for one of the science fiction stories my agent, Kirby McCauley, kept suggesting I should try to write.

The result was "Medusa" (1973), my first novella. Several of my other attempts at science fiction saw even less print than this did, and believe me, no wonder. Whereas I wrote a handful of sword and sorcery tales (not counting the Solomon Kane stories I completed) in order to develop images that seemed too extravagant to be accommodated in my usual stuff, my science fiction stories tried to deal with Themes, too consciously, I feel. "Medusa" is probably the best of them, insofar as here and there imagination surfaces, but I may as well admit that I feel too distant from the story to have any real sense of having written it or of why I did. However, better writers than I have praised it—Dennis Etchison, in his introduction to Bill Munster's three-hundred-copy edition, and T. E. D. Klein—and so they must take some of the responsibility for its presence here.

In 1974 there seemed to be a new market for horror—a bunch of Marvel comics which would include prose tales modelled on the E. C. comics of the fifties. I wrote quite a few that year, appreciating the discipline of having to be terse, even when it transpired that Marvel had decided not to use prose stories after all. "Rising Generation" was my zombie story to go with the other found monsters, and "Wrapped Up" was done for Michel Parry, for a mummy anthology which failed to appear. "Run Through" was based on a dream of seeing a figure repeatedly running towards me, and perhaps the business with the key derives from my own obsessive behaviour: I often have to check several times that I've locked doors or switched off electricity. Writing the story doesn't seem to have helped me stop myself, but the important issue is whether it's a good story. As for "Passing Phase" (also 1974), I've no idea where it came from.

"A New Life" was one of the last of my E. C. pieces. It was written in 1976, the year when much of my energy was devoted to writing novels based on classic Universal horror films. These were published under the house name of Carl Dreadstone—my original suggestion had been Carl Thunstone, but Manly Wade Wellman understandably thought people might assume that pseudonym was his—though in England, to add to the confusion, some were credited instead to E. K. Leyton. I was hoping to reissue my Dreadstone books as an omnibus, but alas, this is not to be. I can at least take this opportunity to make it clear that I wrote only *The Bride of Frankenstein, The Wolfman* and *Dracula's Daughter.* The other novels are nothing to do with me, and by now even Piers Dudgeon, the editor who commissioned the series, can't recall who wrote them.

I suppose both "The Next Sideshow" (1977) and "Little Man" (1978) owe their existence to my liking for fairgrounds and seaside resorts, especially out of season. I live less than half an hour's walk from such a resort, New Brighton. I remember visiting it as a teenager one rainy Boxing Day to see *The Apartment,* Billy Wilder's alleged comedy about attempted suicide, at the moribund local cinema—altogether one of the low points of my life. That I ended up living so close to that setting no doubt says a lot about me.

New Brighton is on the tip of the Wirral Peninsula, and used to be reached by a ferry from Liverpool. "Needing Ghosts" (1989/90) finds a context for my night-time rides on the ferry, along with much that is stranger. I said at the outset that the story was a stage in a process, and for once that was obvious to me during the writing of it. I'd been having problems with my novels: I'd almost blocked at least once while writing *The Influence;* denying myself a psychologically troubled central character in *Ancient Images* had given me more problems than I'd anticipated; *Midnight Sun* gave me several kinds of hell for most of a year. As I was struggling with the latter, Deborah Beale of Legend managed to persuade me to commit myself to following it with a novella, and "Needing Ghosts" was the result, for which my bookseller friend John Mottershead lent me his surname. It may be the strangest piece I'll ever write.

Some of its energy derives from the excitement of working in a form new to me (as distinct from "Medusa," which ended up as a novella rather than setting out to be one). However, that doesn't quite explain why it was such fun to write. Once I'd written the early scene at the bus terminal—more precisely, the bit with the destination indicators—the story kept coming out so much stranger than I could have predicted that I could hardly wait to write it so as to find out what happened next. The process felt immensely liberating, perhaps because I was able to include elements which had seemed too dark for inclusion in *Midnight Sun*, certainly because the story let me explore the territory where horror and comedy overlap, an exploration which led straight to *The Count of Eleven* and to some extent *The Long Lost* too. Where will those books lead? There's only one way to find out, and that's why I continue to write. May the reader enjoy the results as much as I enjoyed the process.

Ramsey Campbell
Merseyside, England
3 August 1992

† CAT AND MOUSE †

You couldn't say that the house crouched. Yet as we came off the roundabout on whose edge the house stood, and stooped beneath the trees which hung glistening over the garden, I had an impression of stealth. It couldn't be related to anything; not the summer glare nor the white house within the garden. But silence settled on us, and the circling cars hushed. And although the sunlight glittered on the last raindrops dripping from the leaves, a waiting shadow touched us and the quiet in the garden seemed poised to leap.

I had to struggle with the key in the unfamiliar lock; my wife Hazel laughed, annoying me a little. I'd wanted to throw the door wide and carry her in, enjoying my triumph; God knows I'd gone through enough to buy the house. But at least I enjoyed her delight once I managed to open the door.

We'd seen the house before, of course, when we were furnishing the rooms, but now we both felt a shock of unfamiliarity. The white telephone amazed us; so did the stairs, a construction of treads like the tail of a kite which was the major addition we owed to the previous tenants. Hazel's was the reaction I could have predicted; she rushed through the downstairs rooms and then clattered upstairs, eager to own the rest of the house. As I watched her run up the open stairs I felt a dull surge of desire. But when I made my own tour of the pale green living-room, the white kitchen cold as a hospital, the bathroom with its abstract blocks of colour and its pink pedestal, I felt imprisoned. The air smelled slightly dank, like fur. Of course Hazel had been wearing her sheepskin coat, but it seemed odd that the entire ground floor should smell of wet fur, a smell that trailed with me like a cloak. I began to open windows. Perhaps, since we'd lived on a third floor for years, I simply needed time to adjust to entering a house whose windows weren't open.

I found Hazel within a maze of double-jointed lights and drawing-board and cartons of books, in the room we'd decided to use as an attic. The smell was stronger here. "Come down and I'll make some tea," she said.

"Just let me tidy up a little."

"You've done enough for a while, love."

"You mean selling myself?" I said, thinking of my ideas and my art which I'd battered against the advertising agency where I worked until they had been battered half out of shape.

"No, I mean selling your talent," Hazel said, then

with an edge of doubt: "You do like our house, don't you?"

"Of course I do. That's why I worked to buy it," I said and stopped, peering down at the windowsill. We had liked the rough wood of that sill, and had left it unpainted. But now, trying to peer closer without appearing to do so, I saw that the sill looked chewed. Or clawed. The former owners must have had a cat or a dog. That was the explanation, yet I was disturbed to think that they had locked it in here, for nothing else could have driven it to such a frenzy that it would have left its claw-marks on the sill and even in the putty round the window-pane.

"I'm sure you'll sleep now that we're here," Hazel said, and I started. "What are you looking so worried about?" she said.

I was thinking how, when I'd stripped the attic to paint it, I had noticed claw-marks tearing through the wallpaper without realizing until now what they were, but I didn't want to upset her; besides, I wished she wouldn't probe me so often, even though it was out of love she did so. "I'm wondering where the stereo is," I said.

"It must be on its way," she said. "They'll take care of it. They can see how expensive it is."

"Yes, well," I told her, faintly annoyed that I should feel bound to explain this point again, "it's the most sensitive. You have to pay for sensitivity."

"I know you do," she said smiling, and I realized she'd found another meaning, a personal meaning which she wanted to share with me. Sometimes her insistence on puns infuriated me; often it made me love her more. I coaxed my gaze away from the patch

21

on the wall where the paper had been clawed. "I wouldn't mind dinner," I said.

The stereo arrived after dinner, halfway through my third cup of coffee. The workmen were clearly annoyed that I should supervise them, as if I were showing them how to do their job. But it was only a job to them; to me it was perfection in jeopardy. When they'd left I played *Ein Heldenleben* at full volume, caring nothing for the neighbours, since they were beyond the garden. Hazel listened quietly, more in order not to disturb me than out of a genuine response to the music. Somehow I felt trapped; the Strauss surged against Hazel's tranquil uncommunicative face, against the padded silence of the room, and never broke. I crossed to the windows and flung them high, and the feeling streamed out into the dark garden, where its remnants clung to the trees.

That night I could neither make love nor sleep. Outside the bedroom window cars whirred lingeringly by, like a sound by Stockhausen passing across speakers. My wife slept buried in the pillow, frowning, her thumb in her mouth. The tip of my cigarette glowed and reddened the landing; it opened in the gloss of the doors like a crimson eye, watching from the attic and from the other bedroom whose purpose was beginning to seem increasingly futile. I had meant to go downstairs, but down there or in my ears lay a faint ominous hiss, quite unlike the threshing of the leaves above the garden. I listened for a few minutes, then I scraped my cigarette on the ashtray by the bed and pulled the covers up.

Hazel woke me at noon. I gathered she'd awoken only recently herself. I unstuck myself from sleep and followed her downstairs. I must have looked disgruntled, judging by Hazel's glances at me. I felt she'd woken me up merely for company. When we reached the living-room she said: "Darling, listen."

I heard only the words, which were the formula she used when she wasn't sure that I would agree. Of course her tone implied another meaning, but I wasn't awake enough to notice. "What is it?" I demanded.

"No, *listen*."

That was the second half of the formula. I often spent an hour before sleep juggling ideas and an hour after breakfast waking up; nothing angers me more than to be called upon to make a decision before I'm awake. "Look," I said, "for Christ's sake, now that you've dragged me out of bed—"

Then I saw that she had been gazing at the stereo. From its speakers came a sound like the hiss of a hostile audience.

"You see, it moves back and forth," Hazel said. "The stereo must have been on all night. Will it have gone wrong?"

"I take it you've left it on to make sure it will?" I couldn't tell her that I wasn't shouting at her but at something else, because I didn't care to admit it to myself. But as I pulled out *Ein Heldenleben* and almost ripped it with the stylus I felt the movement of the hiss, felt it loom like a lurking predator, an actual dark phys-ical presence, as it crept from one speaker to another. Then the Strauss rushed richly out. It sounded perfect, but aside from that it meant nothing. I took it off, scowled at Hazel and stumped back to bed.

I was running upstairs, and the stairs tilted steeply like a ladder. Suddenly sliding gates clanged shut at both ends of the staircase, and something groped hugely through the wall and felt around the trap for me. I awoke struggling. The blanket lay heavy and fluid on my body like a cat, and my skin prickled with what felt like the memory of claws. I threw off the blanket and sat up.

For a moment I was lost; I stared at the blue walls, the grey wall, the impossible silence. I struggled to my feet and listened. It was five o'clock, and there should have been more sound; Hazel should have been audible; the silence seemed charged, alert, on tiptoe. I made my way downstairs, padding carefully. I didn't know what I might find.

Hazel was sitting in the living-room, a book in her hand. I couldn't tell whether she'd been crying; her face looked scrubbed as it would have if she had wept, but I was confused by the thought that this might be the impression she had contrived for me. More disturbingly I felt that something had happened to change the silence while I had been asleep.

She came to the end of a chapter and inserted a bookmark. "I like to sleep too, you know," she said.

"No doubt," I said, and that was that. Through dinner we didn't speak, we hardly looked at each other. It was less that each of us was waiting for the other to speak than as if the silence itself was poised to pounce on the first to succumb. Several times I was almost frightened enough to speak, so that at least my fears might be defined; but each time I determined that it was up to Hazel to begin.

I don't know what music I played after dinner; I recall only visualizing fists of sound crudely battling the blankets of silence. I looked at Hazel, who was trying to read against the barrage of noise which for the moment had lost all meaning. I felt grief for what I might be beginning to destroy. "I'm sorry," I said. "Maybe I'm starting to crack up."

Sometimes Hazel would dodge around the bedroom and I, having pinned her to the bed, would rape her; we seemed to need this more and more often. But tonight we waltzed gently over each other, exploring delicately, until I was too deep in her to need ornamentations. "You're a deep one," I said.

"What, love?" she gasped, laughing.

But I could never offer her puns more than once, and now less than ever, for my body had stiffened and chilled. Perhaps, despite her reassurances, I was cracking up. I knew that at that moment I was being watched. I peered down into Hazel's eyes and tried to gaze through them, and as I felt her nails move on my back I remembered the sensations of claws at the end of my dream.

The next day, Monday, I came home tired by a lunch which one of our clients had bought me; my constant smile had felt more like a death-grin, and certainly had expressed as little emotion. Returning to the agency I'd walked through shafts of envy which had penetrated even my six whiskies. Our house should have offered peace, but all I felt as I opened the front door was the taut snap of tension. I felt awaited, and not only by Hazel.

In the early evening cars passed with a muffled undulating hum, but soon faded. I remembered that back at our flat we could always hear the plop of a tap like a dropper or the echoing cries of children in the baths across the road. Here in the house the silence seemed worse than ever, threatening to drown us, and our speech was waterlogged. Yet it wasn't the silence I found most disturbing. Over dinner and afterwards, as we sat reading, I glimpsed an odd expression several times on Hazel's face. It wasn't fear, exactly; I should have described it as closer to doubt. What upset me most was that each time she caught me watching her, she quickly smiled.

I couldn't stop thinking that something had happened while I had been at work. "How was our house today?" I asked.

"It was fine," she said. "Oh, while I was out shopping—"

But I wouldn't let her escape. "Do you like our house, then?" I asked.

"What do you think?"

I was certain now that she was hiding something from me, but I didn't know how to find it. She could elude my questions by any number of wiles, by weeping if necessary. Frowning, I desisted and put Britten's *Curlew River* on the stereo. Of all Britten's work I love the church parables more than any; their sureness and astringency can make me forget my crumpled colleagues at the agency and their clumsy machinations. I thought *Curlew River* might help me define my thoughts. But I didn't get as far as the second side, with its angelic resolution. Peter Pears' eerie vocal glissandi in the part of the madwoman chilled me like the howls of a sad cat; the church which the stereo re-created seemed longer and more hollow, like a tunnel gaping invisibly before me in the air. And the calm silences with which Britten punctuates his parables seemed no longer calm. They seemed to pounce closer and to grow as they approached. Determined to respond to the music, I closed my eyes. At once I felt a dark stealthy shape leap at me between the music. My eyes started open, and I glanced to Hazel for some kind of support. The room was empty.

And it was dark. On the wall opposite me the wallpaper hung clawed into strips. It was not the living-room. Perhaps I cried out, for I heard Hazel call "Don't worry, you're all right," and something else inaudible. I saw that the wallpaper was after all not clawed, that it was merely shadows that had made it seem so. Then Hazel came in with a tray.

"What did you say?" I demanded.

"Nothing," she said. "I crept out to make some coffee."

"Just now, I mean. When you called out."

"I haven't said a word for ten minutes," she said.

After Hazel had gone to bed I stayed downstairs for an hour of last cigarettes and fragments of slogans. The month looked slack at the agency, but I couldn't stop thinking, and I preferred not to think about the house. Eventually, of course, the house overtook my thoughts. All right, I argued in mute fury, if I were moved by Britten's melodious angels then I might as well admit to a lurking belief in the supernatural. So the house was haunted by the presence of a dog or, as I sensed intuitively, a cat: so what? It didn't worry me, and Hazel hadn't even noticed. But if my grudging belief was the latest fashion in enlightenment, the retreat from skepticism, it didn't seem to be helping me. Spec-

27

tral cats could have nothing to do with my hearing Hazel's voice when she hadn't spoken. I felt that my mind was beginning to fray.

A paroxysm of dry coughs persuaded me to stub out my cigarette. I threw the scribbled scraps of paper into the fireplace and came out into the hall. As I turned out the light in the living-room, a shadow leapt from the hall to the landing with a single bound.

Of course I wasn't sure, and I tried to be less so. I crept upstairs, feeling my heels hang over the open treads of the staircase. For a moment my nightmare returned, and I was heaving myself up a tilted ladder which grew steeper as the gaps between the treads widened. Halfway up I could hear myself panting with exhaustion, perhaps from lack of sleep. At the top the shadows crowded indistinguishably. On tiptoe, I opened the bedroom door. I had drawn it back only inches when a fluid shadow rippled through the crack into the room.

I threw the door open, and Hazel jumped. I was certain she had, although it might have been the bedroom light jarring her blanketed shape into focus. As I undressed I watched her, and after a minute or two she shifted a little. Now I was convinced that she hadn't been asleep when I entered, and was still only pretending. I didn't try to make sure, but it took me some time to turn out the light and slip into bed. For minutes I stood staring at Hazel's obscured body, wondering where the shadow had gone.

I awoke feeling lightened. The room gave out its colours brilliantly; beyond the window waves of leaves sprang up glowing in the sun. It was only as sleep began to peel back a little that I wondered whether Hazel's absence had lightened me.

Once downstairs I didn't go to her. Instead I walked dully into the dark living-room and slumped on the settee. I began to wonder whether I was afraid of Hazel. Certainly I couldn't talk to her about last night. My eyes began to close, and the living-room darkened further. Shadows striped the wall again; in a moment the wallpaper might peel. Or a claw might tear through— The door gushed light and Hazel came in, carrying plates of breakfast. She smiled when I leapt to my feet, but I wasn't greeting her. The living-room was bright, as it had been since I'd entered. I had realized whom I might see. After all, the house was his responsibility.

"How do you feel?" I said, staring into my coffee then glancing up at her.

"All right, love. Don't start worrying about me. I should try and have a rest today if I were you."

I didn't know whether the shadow was speaking; in any case, I resented the implication that I looked incapable. "I'm going to take a couple of hours off this morning," I said. "If you want to come—I mean, if you want to get away from the house for a while—"

"Silly," she said. "You'd be upset if dinner wasn't ready."

My suspicions were confirmed. I couldn't believe that she wouldn't take the chance to escape the house unless it had infected her somehow. I was glad that I hadn't told her where I was going. I managed to kiss her, forgetting to notice whether the feel of her had changed, and hurried round the corner to the car. Muffled thunder hung in the air. For a moment I regretted leaving Hazel alone, but I was afraid to return to the house. Besides, perhaps she was past rescuing. I drove blindly around the roundabout, not looking at the house, and was at the estate agent's within half an hour.

I had forgotten that the office wouldn't be open. I had a cup of coffee and a few cigarettes in a café across the road, and by the time the estate agent arrived I had perfected my smile and my story. A faint astringent scent clung to him, and he pulled at his silver mustache more often than when first I'd met him. I convinced him that I had merely been passing, but still he drew his rings nervously from his fingers and paced behind his desk. At last I fastened on the shrill garrulous couple who had been leaving as I entered, and guided the conversation to them.

"Yes, abominable," he agreed. "I suppose I dislike people. I decided to live with cats a long time ago. People and dogs can be led where cats can't. You'd never train a cat to salivate at your whim."

"Were there cats in our house?" I said.

"Have you been dreaming?" he demanded.

"Just a feeling."

"You're right, of course," he said. "To me, you know, the most frightful act is to kill or maim a cat. Don't offer me Auschwitz. People aren't beautiful. Auschwitz was unforgivable, but there's nothing worse than a man who destroys beauty."

"What happened?" I said, trying to be casual.

"I shan't go into detail," he said. "Briefly, your predecessors were obsessed with pests. One mouse and they were convinced the house was overrun. There are none there now, of course. People and cats have one thing in common: they can lose themselves in their

30

own internal drives to the exclusion of morality, or reality for that matter."

"Go on," I said.

"Well, these people left five cats in the house without food while they went away on holiday. Starve a cat to kill a mouse, you see—as stupid and vile as that. Somehow the attic door closed and trapped the cats. When our friends returned they opened the front door and one cat ran out, never to be seen again. The others were in pieces in the attic. Cannibalism."

"And no doubt," I said, "if someone exceptionally sensitive were to take the house—"

"Yourself, you mean?"

"Yes, perhaps so," I said defensively. "Or for that matter, if one left some piece of sensitive electrical equipment running—"

"I don't pretend to know," he said, but there was despair around his eyes. "Ghosts of cats? I'll tell you this. People underrate the intelligence of cats simply because they refuse to be taught tricks. I think the ghosts of cats would play with their victims for a while, as revenge. Sometimes I wonder what I'm doing in this job," he said. "You can see I don't care."

When I left I drove slowly through the city, thinking. The lunchtime crowds eddied about me; eventually the thickening sky above the roofs was split by lightning, and gray rain leapt from the pavements, washing away the crowds. I drove on as the rain smashed at the windscreen. "Playing with their victims"—there was something to which that was the key. If I were to believe in ghosts, however absurd it seemed beneath the tic of traffic lights, I might as well accept the idea of possession. Was the house playing us as hunter and

31

victim? But I couldn't altogether believe that one's personality could be ousted; I could imagine a framework within which this might be logical, but I wasn't sure that I felt it to be real. Yet I noticed that here, caged in by ropes of rain, I still felt more free than recently: free of the house's influence.

Suddenly I wanted to be with Hazel. If I had to I would drag her out, whatever was within her, however dangerous she might be. I could telephone my agency when I arrived at the house. I turned my car and it coursed through the pools of the city.

Along the carriageways out of the city the trees looked bedraggled and broken. Occasionally I passed torn cars, steaming where they'd skidded in mud. I was hardly surprised, when I reached the house, to see that the telephone wire had snapped and was sagging between the roof and the trees in the garden. As I drove past the roundabout it occurred to me that if Hazel were a victim she was trapped now. She would have to admit that she was as vulnerable as me. No longer would I have to suffer the entire burden of disquiet.

I think it was not until I got out of the car that I perceived what I had been thinking. I felt a chill of horror at myself. I loved her hands on my back, yet for a while I had turned them into claws. All along Hazel had been frightened but had tried to hide her fear from me. That was the doubt that I'd seen in her eyes. At once I knew what had blinded me, what had sought to destroy her. The rain dwindled and the sun blazed out; a rainbow lifted above the carriageway. I rushed through the garden, lashed by wet leaves, and dragged open the door to the house.

The house was dark—darker than it should have

been now that the sun had returned. It was dim with stealth and silence. There was no sound of Hazel. I hurried through the ground floor, stumbled upstairs and searched the bedrooms, but the house seemed empty. I gazed down from the landing and saw that the front door was still open. I was ready to run out and wait for Hazel outside, yet I couldn't rid myself of the impression that the staircase was far longer and steeper than I remembered. Trying to control my fears I started down. I was halfway down when a shadow crept across the carpet in the living-room.

For a moment I thought it was Hazel's. But not only did its shape relate to something else entirely—it was far too large. I stood on the edge of the stairs. If I ran now, whatever was moving in the dim room might misjudge its leap. I wavered, fell down two stairs and jumped clumsily to the hall. At that moment the telephone rang.

In my terror I could see it only as an ally. I backed up the stairs, reached down and caught up the receiver. I muttered incoherently, then I heard Hazel's voice.

"I've got out," she said. "I hoped I might catch you before you came home. Is the door open?"

"Yes," I said. "Listen, love—don't come back in. I'm sorry. I didn't understand what was going on. I blamed you."

"If the door's open you can make it," she said. "Just run as fast as you can"—and then I remembered that the telephone wire was down, remembered the voice that had called to me from the other room.

As I dropped the receiver the air came alive with hissing. It was the sound that the stereo had trapped, but worse now, overpowering. I launched myself from the stairs and came down in the middle of the hall. One more leap and I would be outside. But before I regained my balance I had seen that the front door was closed.

I might have wasted my strength in trying to wrench it open. But although I didn't understand the rules of what was happening, I felt that if the house had tried to convince me that Hazel was safe that meant she was still inside somewhere. Behind me the hall spat. I clutched at the front door. I told myself that I was only using it for support, and turned.

It took me some time to determine where I was. In the dimness the hall seemed green, and a good deal smaller. I might have been in the living-room. But I wasn't, for I could see the stairs; the walls weren't closing like a trap; the shadows hadn't massed into a poised shape, ready to sink its claws into my back. My mind began to scream and scrabble at itself, and I concentrated on the stairs. Eventually, after some hours, the hall imperceptibly altered and seemed stretched to dim infinity. The stairs were miles away. It wasn't worth making for them. There was an acre of open space to be crossed, and I knew I had no chance.

I cried out for Hazel, and from somewhere above she answered my cry.

That cry I knew wasn't faked. It was scarcely coherent, pulled out of shape by terror; it was scarcely Hazel, and in some way I knew that guaranteed its truth. I ran to the stairs, counting my footsteps. Two, and I was on the stairs. I had control of the situation for a moment. I should have kept going blindly; I shouldn't have looked round. But I couldn't help glancing into the living-room.

The doorway was dark, and in the darkness a face

appeared, flashed and was gone, like the momentary luminous spectres in a ghost train. I glimpsed an enormous black head, glowing green eyes, a red mouth barred with white teeth. Then I tore my gaze away and looked up to the landing, and I saw that the stairs had become a towering ladder, a succession of great treads separated by yawning gaps which I could never cross. The air hissed behind me, and I could go neither up nor down.

Then Hazel cried out again. There was only one way to conquer myself, and my mind was so numbed that I managed it. I shut my eyes tight and crawled upwards, grasping each higher stair and dragging myself painfully over space. Beneath me I felt the stairs tremble. I wondered whether they would throw me off, until I realized that something was climbing up behind me. I tightened every muscle of my face to keep my brain from bursting out, and heaved myself upward. I felt a purring breath on my neck, and then I was on the landing.

I stumbled to my feet and opened my eyes. Unless the house was able to blot Hazel from my gaze, she could only be in the one room I hadn't searched, the attic. As I ran across the landing, a huge face flashed at the top of the stairs. Its eyes gleamed with bottomless hatred, and for a second it seemed to fill with teeth. Then I had reached the attic and slammed the door.

I slumped. The attic was so crowded with lamps and cartons that nobody could have hidden there. The objects massed, suffocated and strung together by cords of dust; I didn't see how I could even make my way between them. I might be trapped in the maze and cut off from Hazel, if indeed she were in the room. I knocked one of the looming cartons to the floor in an attempt to clear the view, and on the thud of the carton I heard breath hiss in muffled terror.

At once the room rearranged itself, and I saw Hazel. She was crouched in a corner, her knees drawn up to her chin, her arms pressed tight over her face. She was sobbing. I moved gently towards her, loving her, bullying the fear from my mind. My feet tangled in wire. I looked down and saw the cord for the lamps. I knew where the socket was; I plugged in the lamps and let them blind the door. Then I went to Hazel.

"Come on, love," I said. "Come on, Hazel. We're going now. Come on, love."

Her arms drew back from her face. She looked up at me; then she shrank into the corner and her eyes gaped in horror. I fell back. But her lips moved. She was trying to speak to me. She wasn't frightened of me. I looked behind me, towards the door.

The door had opened, and the doorway was half-filled by an enormous face. Its mouth yawned wide and a tongue sprang dripping across its teeth. I grabbed the lamps and shone them into its eyes, but they didn't blink. Its face began to bulge in through the doorway, and behind it others leapt across the landing to hover grinning above the first. With a surge of pure energy and terror I hurled the lamps at the faces.

What happened I don't know. I never heard the lamps strike the floor. But the surge of energy carried me across the room to heave the window open. I ran to Hazel and pulled her to her feet, although she shrank sobbing into the corner. I threw her across my shoulder and staggered with her to the window. I glanced back into the room, where faces with gleaming eyes capered in the air and flew at us in a single toothed mass. Then I jumped.

I think the house must have overlooked that. Mice might fall from a window, but they aren't supposed to jump. So I spent time in hospital with a broken leg, while Hazel was furious enough by the end of the week to visit the estate agent's. Once she had made him admit that he wouldn't spend a night in the house, the rest was easy. "I have no time for horror," he told her. My leg soon improved. Not so Hazel's insomnia; and yet when we lie awake together talking through the uneasy hours, I think there are times when we're grateful. Somehow we could never talk that way before.

† MEDUSA †

For Doug and Lynne Winter—
a glimpse of a career
that almost was.

I

The shipmen from the *Argosy* had unloaded the supplies and were standing around impatiently waiting for me to say bye. Then Caz came over and took me aside for a moment. His clothes and face looked squashed beneath his snapsuit, earnest in a crumpled way. "You could tell them you've changed your mind," he said. "They survived without you until now. This world won't be good for you. I feel it."

"I thought feeling was my job," I said. I wasn't really laughing at him, and he made me feel less bitter than I sounded.

"It is your job, An, too much so. You let yourself feel without thinking. You haven't thought what life on Fecundity will be like, I don't believe you have."

"Just two men and a worldful of lizards and me, you mean?" I said, catching the image as he thrust it away. "I know one thing, I'd rather have it than another year on ship. Even with you," I added, because I shared a little of his sadness; we'd paired a few times.

"Forget me. I know that wasn't important," he said, and I felt him trying to outdistance his self-pity. "*Argosy-18* will be docking here in a few weeks. You could join that if Fecundity's not what you expect. Just don't let them get too much of a hold on you until you're sure."

I said bye and watched them leave. Several Fecunds, their bodies the bright green that I'd been told denoted early adolescence, had gathered at the edge of the jungle. They sucked the sap from a tubular vine and watched the boat dwindle toward the *Argosy*. I realized that I might miss Caz. He'd volunteered to help transport the supplies. Whether he's pilot or steward or, like Caz, a cook, no shipman likes to descend from his ship to a world and its uncontrolled environment. For most shipmen a world is a dirty joke they have to be paid well to visit. That Caz had volunteered and more, had stayed to talk to me meant we'd shared an essence. And of all places, on an *Argosy*.

The Fecunds were looking at the patch the boat had charred. I felt emotion drifting from them, approximately resignation as far as I could tell. I hurried away from them, not because even though only three-quarters grown they were already as tall as me, but because I didn't think I was ready yet to feel them. The gravity was a little less than Earth's or what passes for it, and this combined with the springy braided tangle of pink roots underfoot to buoy me as I went toward the Home.

I had to forget the Code on ship, otherwise I couldn't have done my job. I've never believed in the part about entering buildings, and since they'd left the outest door of the Home open I walked straight in. I peeled off my snapsuit, feeling like a hot raw vegetable, and dropped it in the slot of the sterilizer. Then I opened the inner door and set out to find them.

They were in the bar, drinking from one of the bottles the *Argosy* had sent down. They were sitting on chopped wooden stumps; apart from the white synthetic walls the building was almost entirely furnished from the jungle. Hebby was the smaller wiry man, not as tall as me, four decades and maybe half, a face like a wedge ragged with graying hair at the wide end, a sharp cold expression. Dack was large-boned and approaching three decades like me, and his flesh gave the impression of having melted slightly, especially his face which seemed to hang a little apart from the skull. The climate had crimped his skin as if he'd been immersed in water. Both of them wore only shorts. I looked at them and at the shoulder-to-shoulder sections of green trunk which were the bar, and at the arcs of wall full of shelves of carved roots and glazed flowers all priced for visitors, and I nearly walked out again. The room was brimming with resigned despair. I caught hold of my mother, shining deep within my mind, and stood where I was.

"We didn't know if you were coming so we started celebrating," Hebby said. "Get yourself a glass."

"I hear you make your own wine."

"Fecundity wine," Dack said, snorting the *f* through

his lips. "You don't want that when we've got the real ship brew."

"She can have some if she wants some," Hebby said, and I did. It was strong with a dry harsh taste that suddenly exploded into sweetness. "Good," I said. "*Argosy-18*'s on the way here, full of visitors. We can sell them this."

"They can't have heard about this place," Hebby said. "They'll be the last. The word's been broadcast, be sure. Fecundity will be off the visitors' charts in no time."

"What's wrong with it?" I said. I felt a block. Dack was pulling his shorts away from his skin, sweating, his mind chasing its tail: I can't be sure, what will she think, she mightn't understand. I played it by the Code: never release a block, help it to release itself. "Are you too hot?" I said. "Don't mind me."

"It's just, I don't want," he said.

"Don't worry," I said, stripping. "I'm hot too." I was, and I couldn't believe I would be bothering them, closely paired as they were—not surprisingly, since they'd been here alone for almost a year. It didn't worry me; in fact I found it reassuring. One of them thought: I don't care how sensitive she is, she's assuming, and it was gone before I could place it. "What's wrong with Fecundity?" I said, feeling my buttocks spreading on chopped wood.

"The saurians," Dack said.

"He means the Fecunds," Hebby said. "But he's right. You know what happened to your predecessor."

I'd heard. As soon as the Home had been built *Argosy-8* had docked. One of the visitors had whittled himself a spear one night. He'd been drunk and the

41

spear hadn't killed, only wounded a Fecund. Up to then there had been no communication with the Fecunds; they'd watched the landings and the building of the Home with what my predecessor had felt as mild unease and curiosity, nothing significant. But as the spear struck, the Fecund sent out a blast of emotion so intense that the telepath went into shock and everyone else fled to the boats. Not until a doctor from the *Argosy*, his mind deafened by a struggle between a desire to flee and an imperative to stop the agony, tended to the wound did the silent cry of suffering begin very gradually to wane, although not before two of the visitors had attempted suicide. "Which proves intelligence," I said. "A mind that can do that has to be powerful."

"What mind?" Dack said.

"Doesn't follow," Hebby said. "A defense mechanism isn't intelligent. The Fecunds don't achieve anything, they don't try to approach us, they don't build, they've got no art, no technology, nothing. If they're intelligent it's not in the way we understand it or are ever likely to. So we're sitting here guarding them in case someone comes along and hurts them, in which case we run screaming for help. And maybe someone somewhere's trying to put a research team together. We've food and water and whatever the ships trade for souvenirs and accommodation. Seldom come, because nobody wants to stay in a zoo where you can't even poke the lizards."

"Then I don't know why you've stayed," I said. "Especially nor why you needed me. They told me it wouldn't be a cradling job, so I can't be supposed to look after you. But we aren't authorized to try to communicate with the Fecunds."

"We've reasons that I think will interest you," Hebby said, and the despair in the room lifted for a moment. "They'll take some explaining. Have another drink for now."

I felt them thinking of each other in case I tried to search. I couldn't feel any hint of a threat to me, so I drank.

Later they showed me my room, which was dominated by two wedged sections of trunks between which a hammock was slung. They'd hung the carriers full of my personals, such as they were, on the branches. Hebby showed me where the best shelves and niches were until I told him I would like to find my own. Dack shifted about in the doorway, mumbling that maybe they could knock out the trunks and trade for some shelves and a bunk next time an *Argosy* docked. "If we're still—" he said, truncated by a glare from Dack and hurried mutual passionate thoughts. Eventually I shooed them out and began to arrange my personals on the trunks.

Then I decided to see a little of Fecundity. I knew I wouldn't sleep much during my first night on a world, not with the feverish heady sensations of lessened gravity and the wine as well. It didn't seem long since I'd sloughed my snapsuit, but the sterilizer warning light was off. I unfolded the suit, made sure it was skin-side in and easing my toes into the feet, pulled it up. As usual I shuddered involuntarily as it snapped shut over my head, but anything's better than a space-suit.

I'd taken the lenses out of the returns shelf of the sterilizer and was clipping them into my eyes when Hebby and Dack emerged from their room. Like mine, it opened off Welcome. They saw me through the open inner door. "We can't be that intolerable," Dack said.

"I just wanted to have a walk around."

"Show her," Dack said. "It's not far."

"There is something you ought to see," Hebby said. "Before you get any false ideas about Fecundity."

I'd wanted to try to walk myself into the rhythm of Fecundity but I couldn't very well refuse. Besides, I'd half-intended to ask if they would accompany me, although I told myself I could handle the elation my new experience might induce, even the increase in oxygen over shipboard air. "You could sort the visitors' guides if you liked," Hebby said to Dack. "Anyway, we won't be long."

"I know that," Dack said. "There's no call for you to worry."

"Well, you know you wouldn't want to come."

"Sooner go, sooner back," Dack said, frowning.

We emerged into the clearing around the Home. It looked odd, the bald patch of ground extending away four or five hundred yards on each side until it met the jungle. Before they'd built the Home, Argosies had razed the area, grubbed out all the roots and sterilized the ground, then slipped sheets of synthetic beneath it to abort anything they'd missed. In one or two places I could see the synthetic like exposed bone, and a few greenish-yellow shoots had poked their way up between the sheets. "No danger there," Hebby said. "We can beat the jungle any time we have to."

We made for the gap in the edge of the jungle where the Fecunds had pushed their way through to watch the departure of the boat. It was cooler now, and the sky was tinted a brilliant lemon I could taste. We entered the jungle and I felt as if I'd become the tiny anonymous human in the views I'd been shown on ship, put in to communicate perspective. To give myself some control of the situation I began to appreciate the aptness of the names we'd given the towering vegetation: tridents, devil's candles, the green Venus-mounts set in their cushions of tendrils. Then I thought no, someone's with me if I lose control, and I let myself go.

"Dack says all this makes him feel like an insect," Hebby said. "I wouldn't disagree, except that the feeling bothers him."

Something in me kept sailing up to attain the peaks of the jungle. Huge pink arrowheaded blades with red veins swept up from their roots to a sharp clawed point I had to totter dizzily, head strained back, to see. I remembered the roots which had spread their mat from the jungle across the edge of the sterilized land. The corridor we were following joined another wide corridor. Stars of five or six trunks, bright moist yellow sheathed in hard translucent bark, rose together to a high chord of trembling attentuated tips against the sky. I knew there was something on this world I could love.

"This path leads where we're going," Hebby said, indicating the wider corridor. "You can see they use it more."

"Don't you think the paths show intelligence? In the sense that they could just break their way through the jungle instead of keeping to routes?"

"No. Shows instinct and that's all. Listen, don't think I don't know how you feel. Every time I heard we'd met life I used to hope it would be intelligent.

Even when we found they were only animals I used to hope it was a mistake, that it was us not being intelligent enough to understand them. And of course, sometimes it was and no doubt we were better for it when we finally realized. I know you've got to have respect for life. But it's not respect for life if you don't admit that some life doesn't deserve respect, it's idealism and it's dangerous. You shouldn't hurt animals but nor should you respect them, either way you're a traitor to your own race. And what you'll see here is animals with instincts, don't let them delude you. Instincts can be pretty impressive. Did you know that elephants on Earth, the original Earth, used to remember the place where they all went to die? This world may produce an intelligent race someday, but nobody you or I can imagine will see it. Now that's over. What Earth—I mean, where are you of?''

''I'm not at all sensitive about that, quite the contrary,'' I said. ''Earth-7 and I'm glad I'm here.''

''Don't be too glad yet. Dack's Earth-6. They're even more traditionalist there, from what he says. They used to call him Jack. Shows you he wants to leave them behind but he hasn't quite yet. I'm ship. Met Dack on Earth-6 and he told me he was trying to convince himself to work in a Home. There's a few like me each generation, who want life to be a bit messier, a bit unhealthier so we can appreciate health. Saves them having to build quite so many ships.'' He stopped. ''Nothing to worry about,'' he said.

He meant the Fecunds that were approaching up the corridor, two abreast. I was uneasy, certainly, in fact I was dizzy with emotions. Earlier, when I'd seen the young ones on the edge of the jungle, I'd watched them as I would have watched a view, sealed into myself by the newness of Fecundity and the hot/cold sensation of the snapsuit osmosing my sweat. Now I saw them perhaps as they were, plus impressions and hasty approximations: like great pale green conical fruit, the cone's tip drooping (the long-snouted head); no danger, for they simply walked around anything sentient, breaking themselves a wider path if necessary; the base of the cone separated into two heftily muscled trudging legs; hide like a single piece of thick flexible leaf; the left eyelid of one pursing forward to squeeze out of the eye a stray rolling drop of moisture; the pale adults leading, the progressively brighter young behind; their total lack of vocal sound, the thud and crunch of their tread on roots and leaves; the arms of the two leaders stretching out not quite in unison to crack and bend a wider path; the heads going by above me, snouts puckering; an emotion which perhaps wasn't mine but which through the turmoil I couldn't begin to grasp.

"Couldn't you smell it?" Hebby said, taking his hand away from his face where it had cupped him a snapsuited handful of air.

There was a hot sweet slightly excremental odor trailing behind the plodding Fecunds. "Yes, I suppose so," I said, trying to shake my mind free of pejorative words like plodding.

I saw that the arcade of trunks soon opened into what seemed to be a wide field full of low green mounds. Thick broad-leaved yellow grass sprang up again beneath my feet where the Fecunds had passed. What I'd taken to be a moist cluster of fronds on a trunk separated without warning and came at me, beating gauzy wings and gliding. I closed my mouth, temporarily sealing the snapsuit over my lips. Some of the orange glideworms, as my memory named them, brushed against my lenses and I saw the puckered yellow mouth in the tip from which a white tendriled tongue uncoiled, the glideworm's version of an eye. I walked on, feeling sealed into myself again. "There it is," Hebby said.

I opened myself for a moment, then I sealed. The pale almost white green mounds stretched as far as I could see. They reminded me of stories I'd heard of Old Earth, burial mounds, graveyards. And that was what it was, except that the mounds were dead Fecunds lying in the open. Some were piled in heaps from which gas rose, others lay alone. Within the ruptured skin of the one nearest me I could see yellow eggs and movement.

Fallen trees lay among the corpses. In places, branches had punctured skin as they fell. Nearby I saw a Fecund straddling one of the trunks and eating fruit which it had picked from a purple bush growing through a corpse. The Fecund's weight pressed the trunk down, the branches thrust deeper and fluid welled up from a corpse. "I'm going back now," I said, refusing to admit to Hebby that he'd made his point.

He had to lope to catch up with me. "Stay out a few minutes," he said. "There's something else you ought to see. Not unpleasant, and a good deal more interesting."

I could feel him thinking of Dack again in case I glimpsed the display he was preparing. He had the right to a private mind, of course, but people won't realize that the harder they concentrate on something or even on its concealment the more likely it is to be

broadcast in the raw form which makes telepathy un-
avoidable. I was surprised how conscious his thoughts
of Dack were, how much effort he needed to produce
them. There was a sense in which I could take them as
an insult, as an assumption I had to be reminded that
he wasn't interested in me. "That's it," he said.

We'd reached the edge of the Home's patch of
ground. He was pointing to a light which glinted on the
horizon, through the rising mist. "What is it?" I asked.

"The next planet out in this system. When Argosies
were here they had a glance at it, decided it was a form
of quartz, uninhabited. We agree it's uninhabited but
otherwise we think it's a good deal more interesting.
The entire planet's made of it, but we don't think it's
quartz. A metal was your staple on Earth-7, wasn't it?"

"Yes," I said, sealing.

"Then you'll see what I'm thinking. See it intellectually, I mean. There's nothing in the Argosies contract
that says employees can't claim unclaimed territory.
We've been observing it for a year and now we need to
go up and make an analysis. But first we want to find
out something, and that's what you're for."

He'd taken me back to Earth-7 and in my present
mood I didn't feel like forgiving. "What?" I said.

"Aren't you wondering why suddenly you can't see
any Fecunds? As soon as that planet rises they do
that."

After a while I saw where he was pointing. There,
and there, and nearer, the pink arrowheaded blades
had been pulled down to ground level like huge shells.
On some I could just make out the claws of a Fecund,
holding the cover down. In one or two places a Fecund's arm, almost as long as its body, exerted itself

49

against the spring of the leaf. Occasionally it would shift to dig its claws deeper, like an uneasy sleeper's arm on a sheet.

"There's usually something else," Hebby said. "Yes, there. Look!"

One of the leaves sprang erect. Two Fecunds, adolescent green, shuffled rapidly out and stood looking at the gleam on the horizon. Then they hurried back, reached up and hung by their claws on the leaf until it creaked down to cover them.

"The bravado of the young," Hebby said. "We want you to read one of them. Find out what they're thinking about that planet."

"Thinking?" I said, pouncing.

"Dogs can think," he said.

"Perhaps when I can feel the Fecunds as they are," I said. "In time."

I hadn't felt anything from the adolescents. Only a dark cold space or an armour around their minds. Taut glideworms slipped past my face. I watched them fertilizing the round-lipped flowers of a tree as the tree's tenant, a chain of large purple fruit with tendrils, snared them. As I walked away, even the sight of the white cylindrical Home and the snapsuited planethopper and redundant groundcar on the bare plain seemed welcoming.

II

By the time I reached my room I felt nauseous, as much from the cumulative effect of the gravity as anything. I didn't sleep for hours. I lay in the hammock, in the silence between the windowless walls. I felt my mother drifting calmly across the far reaches of my mind like a star sailing on the horizon, and I thought a good deal of this:

Once we began to spread from the original Earth (Old Earth as they call it on its imitators, Earth-O as the shipmen call it) our attitudes had to mature at the speed of our ships. We had to relearn most of them in terms of infinity, and in particular of the infinite variety of life. After the initial few shocks we did so with what I still believe to be admirable determination. The fact that those who couldn't take it were discouraged from leaving Earth helped, of course. Someone must have realized the damage they might do. Instead, contact teams trained in disciplines such as telepathy, comparative culture, comparative psychology and so on were the vanguard, and surprisingly successful too. All this information I found between the lines of a history book which traced our expansion largely through a series of contemporary jokes: "Don't tread on it, federate with it," "Take off those polaroids, I'm saying hello," and the famous one about the benevolent symbionts of Buddha 5, "Don't flush me, I'm your friend."

I say "our" expansion; most Earth-7s wouldn't. Eventually, of course, money overrode the government back on Earth. The industrialists, conscious of having exhausted the world, bought themselves and their employees outward passage. Where they couldn't buy transport they had it built and took the builders with them. They were looking for worlds like Earth, which they could exploit without having to share them with another intelligence. Their surprise was finding so

51

many so easily. Some were colonized direct from Earth, the later ones from their predecessors; all acquired xenophobes from elsewhere. They refused to federate except with each other, but kept to their undertaking not to interfere elsewhere after the horrid example of Earth-3, whose limp attempt at conquest caused it virtually to destroy itself under the aim of pure telepathic paranoia. I don't know how the idea of calling each world Earth began. Since each Earth believes itself a duplicate of the original if not improved and, as Caz confirmed for me, has history books to prove it, I wasn't supposed to know.

Enough perspective. Knowing these things releases me from Earth-7. Now I can look at my life there.

When I was almost five I often used to visit the assessor's shop in our block. There was one in most blocks, particularly later as people realized that instead of haggling over the worth of third-copy Earth facsimiles they could crossbreed plants and sell them for real ones. I don't think it's only my memory that says his shop was smaller and more crowded than the others; already, among the third- and even fourth-copy books and videotapes, there were ranks of potted flowers which between my birthdays would be replaced by their even more baroque offspring. He gave me a book once, and I remember thinking he looked just like the gnome sitting by himself among the foliage in one of the illustrations, except that he didn't smile until he saw me. One day he lifted me up when I came in, and then each time he lifted me higher until behind his action I glimpsed a sad shadowy face peering up my skirt. I screamed, and I never went in his shop again. My mother wanted him publicly whipped, which was a frequent spectacle but which most people believed to be done with a fake hollow whip filled with synthetic blood, though in fact that was very expensive. But my father (I later learned) gave him the address of the local sexbed house, which included childbeds, and the few times I met him after that I sensed embarrassment, not frustrations. After the incident I heard my father say "We should have known." I gathered he meant both the incident and my perception of it.

I began to become aware that words had shadows, often more solid than they. Some of the shadows were so dark that they settled over my mind like webs heavy with soot. I avoided them instinctively and made straight for the light which, I was delighted to find, often grew brighter when people saw me. I used to be sad when it faded and would play, dance, sing, turn somersaults to coax it forth and to express my joy when it brightened. Not too much or I would exhaust it; I became skilled in determining when to stop. But I was convinced that however much it dwindled, even if it shrank to a point so minute I couldn't see it, it was still there and wanted nothing more than to be fanned. That was how I decided to become an actress.

I made that ambition the foundation of my life and I didn't look at it again. I went to school and learned all about Earth-7 and a little about the rest of the universe. I registered as a telepath and learned the Code, one of the few things that had survived intact from the original Earth. Never enter a mind uninvited, a room is the extension of a mind so ask to be let into both, always tell people if they're broadcasting. I even practiced some of it.

My father left us when I was eleven, in pursuit of an affair with the daughter of the family who had the omn synthesizing concession on the far side of the world. His virility made him acceptable to a family threatened with barrenness, though he was paid for it in omn, not as he'd hoped in marriage. Sexual disenchantment leading to barrenness was becoming more widespread on Earth-7. I fanned the single light in my mother's mind, which was me.

I left school six years later and enrolled in creativity college. I was surprised to find I was the only telepath in my year. There had in fact been few in my generation, and progressively fewer after that. I remember having a violent argument about the reasons, with the actor I'd paired with for the course (largely to economize on rent). I was convinced that telepathy involved an attitude of mind and discipline, rather than heredity, and that the decline of this attitude was important enough to analyze seriously, even professionally. I wrote a short play and played in it to our first public at the end of the year. It was a failure.

I left it behind and went through two more years' training. I was sure I could have done it in less time, but as the lone telepath I could hardly expect special treatment. At least I knew that like everyone else I was sure of work at the end. They were often forced to minimize casts in the theatres, even the live-and-hologram horror theatres. They had the subsidies and sometimes the audience, but not the creatives. I managed to join the cast of the largest in New York, the Lovecraft Monster Theatre.

It took me five performances to feel what was wrong strongly enough to leave. I'd been cast as comic relief.

I was a space explorer whose peak scene involved chasing a hologrammatic monster composed largely of hair and synthetic feces around the theatre, shouting ''Come back here, in some ways you remind me of my husband.'' I didn't like it but I had to start somewhere. I felt the way the audience related to the scene and I grabbed hold of it and acted it out. That was what I'd done when I was little, acted out the little girl the adults were seeing. I grasped the heightened image they were seeing and built on that, using their minds as steps to a climax. But then I found that their minds had stopped building. I was trying to climb on nothingness all alone. Ha ha ha ha *ho ho ho* ha ha, clap clap clap ha ha clap clap. I knew the sounds people made when they were enjoying themselves. But I could also look behind the stares and know that the light I'd been trying to fan had gone completely. It hadn't been there at all.

It was here I had to realize that my mind had been so solidly founded that I hadn't even thought to examine my ambition occasionally. Even when I came near, with my notions about the decline of telepathy, I didn't relate the concepts. Now I had to admit an explanation.

It was there all around me: omn. One of those words you can't even remember learning. Scratch the ground almost anywhere on Earth-7 and if it isn't already visible it will be then: omn. I was very young when I learned the definition too: by far the commonest mineral on Earth-7, twice as hard as your fingernail. Add that it can be compounded easily into substances as hard or soft or malleable or whatever as you want. Add further that it is a dull green about the colour of an anonymous paint after years of weathering, and that as if to remind you of their origins the compounds persist

55

in that colour. Consider that it represents I should say three-quarters of what Earth-7s see every day: hills, soil, machinery, even some buildings. And that most of them work with it: my father quarried it, my mother compounded it in the laboratory. Omn: it even sounds as it is, the sound of a heavy gong immediately muffled. All that was why I knew I couldn't stand groping around in the dull green inside people's heads. So I left the theatre, determined for the sake of my clarity of mind to write a book about my revelation.

A year later I tore it up, angry and miserable and aware that I couldn't distinguish the point at which the dulling of my own perceptions began to affect my view of everyone else's. I had to persuade myself of that or accept that every mind on Earth-7 was dark, even those of children. A few weeks later I began to wonder if I could write a novel on all these themes. I tried. Meanwhile I worked cross-breeding flowers, because most people's minds came closest to lighting as they watched the progression of colours. Then I set myself up as an omn creator, which meant learning the elements of sculpture, opening a street stall and sculpting direct from people's minds. It was profitable but more disheartening than the theatre, and I was close to finishing my novel after nineteen months and certain that nobody, even those who didn't specialize in Earth facsimiles, would publish it.

Then my mother died.

Perhaps because we'd grown closer over the years and so I knew where to look for it, or perhaps because I'd devoted myself to it as much for my sake as hers, I could always see the light in her mind when I wanted to, and know it was there even when I didn't call on it.

Sometimes it was set in dull velvety green, but however tiny it was always clear. I was miles away across New York when it went out. It was like going blind, except that everything in the street instantly pressed against my eyes, too close for me to see. I stood and cried out. Then I ran for the El.

As the train rocked I felt as if the light was being jerked out of reach as I clutched at it. I nearly had it, but it was fluttering with panic and slipped away. I forced myself toward calm and let my mind mould to the essence of my mother. I closed my mind about her like hands about a moth and began to project: I'm here, I've got you. I'd hardly ever projected before, except once when she'd heard that someone had fallen from the El and had thought it was me. Now I felt as if I were an armour about her, and projected without thinking. I remembered performing aerobatics for her when I was little. As I remembered, the light grew.

When I reached home all the windows of our terrace were curtained, a hundred of them. They looked separate yet united, and for the first time I noticed there wasn't a green among them. My mother had died twenty minutes ago of a heart attack, I was told. I felt her glowing in my mind. I watched her corpse being borne away and listened to the onomatopoeic gongs in the church and saw the urn carried into the spire for the wind to scatter her ashes, and wondered how soon I could leave Earth-7. I knew I would have to release my mother, but not here. I could already feel her fluttering restlessly then trying to sink back into the depths of my mind. A mind isn't made for two people.

So I went to Argosies. It's an irony so familiar the shipmen don't even bother to repeat it that the planets most dedicated to the idea of their own superiority produce the greatest number of people anxious to travel. The richer you are the younger you go, which of course means that most don't go at all. But the irony is basically false, since the visitors are dedicated to seeking inferiority and return brandishing the most repulsive tales of symbiosis and miscegenation the shipmen can produce or, when necessary, invent. As for the shipmen, given the prices they're paid by the visitors they can even bear to pick them up and deviate a little from their trade routes between the federated worlds and build Homes. Their one notorious problem is the reactions of many visitors to the experience of space. The visitors refuse suspended animation: they may be terrified but they won't be robbed of their journey. Which is why, since my father had been told the secret by a telepath friend, I got the job immediately.

In fact I found the prospect exciting. Now that I'd hastened projecting, which seemed to involve nothing more than rechanneling the subject's thoughts or emotions in terms of the structure of the subject mind, I was anxious to make use of it. More: I felt that in space, if anywhere, I could rekindle the lights I missed, however deep they lay. Space would be my great ally. I donned a waitress' costume in the boat and was enormously excited, as if preparing for a game.

They'd examined me before I was allowed near the boat, but somehow I managed to develop a cold during my first day on ship. The shipmen looked at me in horror and one or two hurried away to be sick. By the time I'd shaken it off and emerged from my cabin, acquiring a coat as I went from a disinfectant spray directed by a snapsuited young shipman, I identified the polarized vistas of space with the floating specks of fever. I levered myself up as best I could through the minds of the shipmen, who had domesticated space as a kind of immense constantly changing hologram. I'd waived the Code in their employ and didn't see why they should be exempt. One or two held potential fear, and I avoided them.

Then I took hold of three of the visitors, much to the surly relief of the shipwoman telepath who had been cradling them all during my fever. ''Usual material. About average,'' she described them. That was why I left the ship. One man was sailing forward helplessly into a gigantic gulping vagina. One woman felt huge white masks peering in the windows behind her. Another man was simply falling, diarrhea and vomit and shame trailing him like a comet's tail. Yet their faces frowned and pouted and strained to smile at the other faces, and didn't even twitch. I felt as if I were groping in the dark and ignored by everyone, in a nursery full of vague giant objects about to tread or fall on me. I groped and turned the first keys I could find: man riding the ship; woman making up in an infinite friendly mirror; man floating on a childhood picture's cloud. Then I left them, returning only in response to alarms. I couldn't inhabit their fears, they were too large and required me to hire out too much of myself without being sure I could retrieve it. I might either numb myself like the shipwoman and risk losing the motivation of my telepathy, or shatter.

Caz helped me. It was Caz who when I came into the visitors' kitchen ashamed and sodden with disinfectant, invisibly so, said, ''You should have seen what they did to me when I came back from Buddha 5.'' It was Caz who watched my playing at being a waitress while I played at cradling the visitors' minds, watched me and sympathized while I played at smiling at the visitors and never having seen them outside the food-room. It was Caz who, one day when my mother was struggling bewildered in my mind while I began to topple into the vagina as the masks peered closer, sat me down and scooped the floored meal into the disposal and cooked the meal again. It was Caz who paired with me to give me a hold in the void, not realizing that I had to battle his dim fear of psychic robbery and castration by my experience of his orgasm. And it was Caz who underwent a spraying as he emerged from the visitors' staff's quarters, and found the Fecundity personnel call near the *Argosy*'s route, and told the bridge I hadn't recovered from the loss of my mother and "you know these telepaths, they have to be like they're made of crystal," all of which I let him believe, and had my contract transferred and arranged for a replacement telepath to be waiting at the next federated dock. All I had to do was grope in the dark a few times and turn the keys tight, and wait for Fecundity.

III

Towards evening some three weeks after my arrival, Hebby was showing me how to clarify the shapes in roots by carving when Dack ran in. "This is it, you won't believe," he said to Hebby. "Come and see."

"He's just showing me," I said, but they'd gone.

60

They came back ten minutes later. "That's it," Hebby said. "Better than we've been waiting for."

"All right, I'll play," I said. "Unless you're going to invite me in."

Hebby's mind clenched protectively around his thoughts. "Shall we tell her?" he said.

"Wouldn't mean anything. You don't know geology, do you?" Dack said to me.

My sciences had grown thinner as I grew older and had snapped long before I left school. Later I associated them with the dull green workday memories in my mother's mind. But I resented Dack's assumption. "You must have the elements in your mind somewhere," I said. "I might just see if I can dig them out and learn that way."

"Don't!" Dack cried, covering his cranium with his hands then pulling them away with an angry rush of dignity.

"She won't," Hebby said, and I shook my head in confirmation. "Listen, An, you'll appreciate this. How would you react to a substance that never stops growing?"

"No way particularly."

"As a creative? You don't see a whole new creativity coming from it? To leave aside the scientific possibilities. I can't even imagine them."

"You're not telling it right," Dack said. "It's that planet you call Eveningstar, An, the one Hebby and me stayed here for. I've been observing it. The structure's crystalline, we told you that. Do you know crystals? Well, I'll try and simplify it for you. They're still growing. I've watched them forcing themselves up through the surface, which is slower. The growth can't be plutonic because they continue to grow on the surface, it isn't magma as I understand it because there's no evidence of heat to speak of, it isn't metamorphic activity because there doesn't seem to be a change in structure."

"Stop showing off," Hebby said. "Straightforwardly, the diameter of Eveningstar has increased while we've been observing it. The planet's growing without releasing any energy that need bother us. We want to take a closer look. But first we want to know quickly what the Fecunds have against it."

"Unauthorized contact is a federal crime," I said. "It's in the Argosies contracts."

"They made you break your Code when you signed that contract," Dack said. "You can't be loyal to them and to what you are. What right do they have to our loyalty? Because there's edible food here they give us hardly any real food. They give us pay which we can't spend here, and not much of that. They don't try to get us visitors. They leave us a planethopper which would get us to three consecutive planets, just about, if we're lucky and they're not too far apart, if trouble broke out here. It won't, but that's not the point. We don't want to hurt the Fecunds. All we want is for you to try to feel what they're feeling." Growing in his mind was a sense of being trapped by jungle, and a broken promise of a holiday.

"Say yes and I'll program the planethopper," Hebby said. "Sooner go, sooner we can file the claim before the next *Argosy* comes in. Each *Argosy* makes it more likely they'll realize that here's a claim worth filing, you know. After your experience I wouldn't have thought you'd have wanted them to have it. And if you're worried that the federal team will find you in the minds of the Fecunds, don't. By the time they arrive, if, we'll be on the other side of space and able to buy them six times over." Eagerness nearing the edge of frustration in his mind.

"I wanted to find out more about the Fecunds first," I said. "I don't know them. But all right, I'll try."

I stood outside the Home while they rushed about, pulling back the snapsuit skin from the planethopper, programming its idiot-savant computer, lifting in the red three-legged globe of the distress signal, loading supplies. A flock of eggbirds, blue ovals with wings and retractable legs, hovered in a down-pointing cone above the jungle. I gazed along the surrounding wall of brilliant intricate rearing bursting vegetation, still but intensely alive in the clear yellow early evening light. "Dack, you attract a Fecund while I finish checking the hopper," Hebby said. "If we wait much longer they'll start covering."

Dack hurried away. "You'd better go with him," Hebby said. "Not too close or they'll just walk round you. A lot of movement at a distance makes them curious. Bring it out where it can see what part of the sky we're pointing at."

It was the first time I'd entered the jungle since Hebby had shown me the field. Since then I'd stood at the edge of the jungle watching the Fecunds, trying to overcome what I'd seen, and of course it had grown in my mind while I searched the Home for jobs the others hadn't already claimed. Dack had already found a Fecund, sucking on a vine. It was a dazzling youthful green and only a little taller than us. Dack was dancing for it. He was more graceful and alluring than I'd ever been.

I joined him and started leaping, somersaulting, handstanding, surprised that I could still do so effortlessly and in a snapsuit too. No doubt it was the gravity. I was handstanding and laughing at the sight of the Fecund like a great green hanging fruit wrinkling its tip when it began to move. I fell, terror rushing through me. Most of it was Dack's. The jungle towered above him, he was an insect about to be trodden. "Hebby wants it right out in the open," I panted, dancing backwards.

The Fecund hesitated at the edge of the razed area, then came on. I had a faint impression of its response to the area, something vaguely approaching an embarrassed giggle. I disliked thinking of the Fecund as *it*, which seemed pejorative and alienating, but whatever genitals it had were hidden in a cleft above its legs. I searched gently for sexual awareness, but the search began to mirror itself at once. "It's no good," I said. "There's nothing I can assume. I can't interpret from nothing."

"Bring it further," Dack said, and his mind pleaded.

The Fecund was plodding stumpily after us, toward the Home. Dust puffed beneath its tread. It was looking at the Home, and its silent giggle continued. Or perhaps my hasty interpretation did. I tried to clear my mind and start again. The impression returned. "Over here," Hebby said from the doorway of the Home.

He shoved me into the doorway, behind the Fecund. "You just feel," he said. "We'll point."

All I could see was the stolid green back of the Fe-

64

cund and squeezed between it and the doorframe, glimpses of Hebby and Dack silently jerking their fingers toward the sky. I closed my eyes. An impression drifted toward my mind and I caught at it. "Lifeless," I said. "Barren. Empty womb."

"Lifeless," Dack muttered. "So much for their prejudices."

"Pairing with stone," I said. "Something like a dirty joke—no, that's probably overinterpretation. Obscene."

The impressions were sailing toward me faster, growing larger, more intense. I had to structure them quickly before they overwhelmed me. "Very approximately, monster story, no, folk tradition, innate knowledge, racial memory perhaps," I stammered to relieve my mind a little. "Giving birth to stone. Fecunds with stone heads. Bare plain. Ranks of Fecunds with their heads lined with stone. What are you doing?"

I'd opened my eyes. The Fecund was shuffling back and forth, trapped. Its skin was moist and working like a grub's. Eveningstar had risen, and Hebby and Dack had closed in so that the Fecund couldn't escape without knocking one of them aside. "Let it go!" I cried, feeling the distress cry beginning within my mind as if all my nerves were a moment away from exploding with pain.

"Not yet," Hebby said. "What else?"

Then the Fecund purged, narrowly missing Dack, who sprang away. At once the Fecund plunged through the gap he'd left and stumped swiftly away, the threat of its cry fading. "Filthy animal," Dack cried. "Filthy, filthy," and he grabbed a sharp tool from beside the planethopper and ran awkwardly after the Fecund.

I interrupted his motivation. He turned blank-eyed then shocked. "You did that," he said.

"And I'd do it again."

"You're more of a woman than she is," Hebby said to Dack. "Put those tools in the hopper and get in. An, one question now and let's get off before we overshoot the program. Then anything you have to say you can say in flight. Did you feel any warning about Evening-star?"

My mind told me that I'd felt the terror of a persecuted adolescent, an adolescent hemmed in by terror. "If I had I don't think I would tell you," I said. "But no. However, I'm not going."

"Please," Hebby said. "We don't know what effect this may have had. They just might turn hostile. Whether the federals arrived in time or not this wouldn't be a place to stay. And we still don't know about Eveningstar. There may still be something there you'd notice where we wouldn't. I don't think you'd want anything to happen to us even now. You may not like what we did but remember, we don't feel as intensely as you." Desperation nearing despair. "We need you," he said.

Fecundity had dwindled to a bright arrested kaliedoscope, to a blur of colours, to a greenish-purple sphere when I said, "All that rushing about was to distract me. And sending Dack into the jungle so I'd feel his fear. It was all planned."

"I'm afraid so," Hebby said, and Dack said, "And

you didn't realize. Shows you're not as sensitive as you like to think.''

IV

When Eveningstar swelled from a globe of milk with a dazzling rim to a white glittering expanse beneath the planethopper I'd lost all sense of time. For me the flight had been measured by silence, and the taste of dehydrates dryly blooming in my mouth, and the slow growth of Eveningstar ahead. Several times I'd felt a tentative remorse reaching toward me from within Hebby's mind then, as his lips pursed to keep it in, falling back. Dack had kept talking geology with him, and eventually began trying to show me the lights and luminous whorls of space streaming past. I put the empty seat between me and the others and leaned my head against the storage compartments, drifting inside myself. I noticed that the computer must have stolen some of their time-sense as well. Long before we reached the point where they would have to take control they were glancing at the chronom.

We were only a few hundred feet above Eveningstar and hovering in search of a hospitable landing when Hebby said for the second time ''No life, you're sure?''

I was observing the landscape, or rather an odd effect it was having on my mind. The eye-filling plain of frozen milk, translucently frosted on the surface with paler crystals, the hint of a pattern where light caught a curve of crystal faces, a pattern something like interlocking and overlapping cogs, all this persisted briefly in my mind even when I looked away, like the image of bright light on the retina. "No life," I said.

The planethopper bumped down, shifted slightly and settled. My mind produced the crackle of upthrust crystals pulverizing beneath our weight. I could feel Dack's refreshment as the still glazed plain erased the rioting colours and textures of Fecundity from his mind. From Hebby came only control so powerful it felt like an unbroken sphere.

The sun rested on the horizon. Its rays struck the tips of crystals and shattered them into colour. The plain was strewn with sparks that seemed to hover just above it, blue, pale green, violet, coldly burning red. Further off they hung in a packed band of throbbing colour, and beyond was gray dimness. I opened myself to the sight but was surprised, even granting my awareness of the intervening polarized windows, to find that my emotions weren't touched. My mind kept trying to fix the point at which the separate static explosions of light merged into the vibrating band, and that was all.

Dack had put his arm around Hebby's shoulders and was pointing at the spectacle of the landscape. Desire was fretting in his mind, mute because aware of me behind his head like a hindering shadow. Hebby was aware of me in a way that he, therefore I, couldn't define. I felt his resigned acknowledgment of Dack's smothered longing. "We should sleep now," he said. "One good day's work tomorrow and we can be away and ahead."

My mind felt light and difficult to weigh down with sleep, and besides I knew why he wanted me asleep. I almost said: can't you two feel a bit more quietly? But if I saw no reason not to say it I also saw no reason to suffer the argument which would no doubt ensue. They must know they broadcast sometimes, I thought, it's all a game in which we have to pretend we don't know we're playing it. I'm best sitting out. I reclined my chair and closed my eyes.

I was huge and slowly rolling. It took me a long time to awake, because I had to pull myself up through several layers of awareness. The surface, an oppressive crust I had to battle through, was a sense of impotence like that I'd received from Caz while pairing but far worse, stifling. I withdrew from it far enough to see that it came from Hebby, and then I was fully awake. "See, it was her," I heard Dack say above me. "There, you can see she's only pretending to be asleep."

I opened my eyes before I was blinded and deafened by impotence and rage. Hebby was waiting in front of them, and as soon as they opened his face swelled with blood. "So it was you," he said. "That much is in your face. What's the matter, jealous? Do you want some too? I'm ready any time, be sure."

"I'll hold her," Dack said.

"Don't be stupid," Hebby said. "What makes you think I'd need that? Of course, she's making you think so."

I knew I could trace their hatred to its roots and snap it off. But I also knew instinctively that I mustn't manipulate Hebby's mind or his still controlled rage and disquiet would spill out, scalding us all. Instead I made straight for the defensiveness which his words only partly concealed. "Please don't let Dack do this to me," I said. "I really was asleep until you woke me.

I'm not jealous of anyone. I just wanted to be some-where I didn't need to relate very much. I was glad you two were paired. I just wanted to work and maybe even try not to be a telepath for a while."

"You can't believe her," Dack said. "You can feel her all the time, making you have to shrink so she can't see you. It's like the jungle. She doesn't have to do anything, you can always feel her there."

"I never knew you felt that way," I said. I'd felt his fear that I might steal Hebby, but nothing else. I'd been going blind and hadn't realized.

"Never knew!" Dack shouted. "Listen to her!"

"I don't think she did," Hebby said, gazing at me. "Any more than I did."

"I'm sorry if I haven't let you know me," I said. "I know I've just helped and done jobs and not made myself clear. If I'd known you weren't seeing me I'd have been clearer. But at least it shows I'm not what you think I am. If I had been I'd have known to protect myself." I was surprised how true all this was. I was at the same time disturbed to feel my face and body shifting about to express my conviction. My face felt like a mask I was clumsily trying to sculpt. I saw my head sinking, my expression drooping. My mind was threatening laughter. Instead, I managed to reenter myself enough to weep.

"She's trying to say she isn't affecting us," Dack said.

"Obviously I am," I said. "But I don't mean to. I wouldn't have any reason to inhibit you. It's probably just my being here that did it. And you can't expect me to do anything about that."

"It doesn't matter if I believe you or not," Hebby

70

said, and he'd sphered himself again. "But I must behave as if I do, otherwise this flight will be a disaster. Same for you, Dack. Leave her alone from now on. Remember why we're here and let's stay ahead of Argosies." He lay back in his chair and so did Dack eventually, frowning. But I felt them both waiting for me to fall asleep before they relaxed their minds.

In the morning I awoke first, forcing myself up through sleep like layers of melted cheese. I set out dehydrates and a tube each of juice. When Hebby and Dack awoke they grinned in embarrassment and ate silently. I did catch a faint suspicion from Dack that I'd tampered with the dehydrates, before he dismissed the idea as absurd. I gazed out onto the plain, where light lay jagged as lightning along the highest tips of crystal.

Then it was suiting time. I found I'd still been hoping that we could survive with snapsuits, quite irrationally since the mass of Eveningstar could hold little atmosphere. I cradled my helmet in my hands and stared at it. "Aren't you ready?" Dack said. "Sooner go, further we're ahead." I screwed it into place and at once my world sounded like the inside of a balloon, and my breathing as if my lungs were pressed against my ears, inflating into them. My flesh squirmed between bone and suit. Nevertheless, I pulled the suit hood over the top of the helmet and sealed them together.

Descending was the worst part: not being able to feel the rungs of the ladder through the thick synthetic soles, risking loss of foothold by trying to see through the too slightly inclined helmet how securely planted my feet were. Then we were down and beginning to walk, and already a somewhat nauseous euphoria was uncoiling in me. Because the spacesuit billowed slightly and plucked at me like a loose skin, while I felt as though floating within it. Because of the sight of the pumped-up figures of Hebby and Dack ahead, each hobbling as if his ankles were chained closely together. Because of the landscape gliding sluggishly by like a retarded silent videotape to which my sucking whistling breath had been added as accompaniment. Because of the way colours stirred and faded above the motionless creamy landscape as I moved, while further off the plain seemed to crack with outlines of light. Because I couldn't relate to the landscape in any way: the fact that I called it motionless proved that. Because, shuffling along above this unheard unfelt world, I felt as if my mind were drifting loose from everything.

A tiny Hebby was squeaking against my ear. ''Dack, don't be afraid to go too slow. An, looks like a slippery incline ahead of you. Don't fall but if you do, remember to get your elbows down. They're reinforced for it. Field of very thin crystals ahead, Dack, you can't see them from your angle. Good for samples but don't put your weight on them. Anything interesting, An?'' He kept asking me that in what I knew was an attempt to include me, which only made me feel more excluded. I knew my usefulness had ended once I'd confirmed there was no life.

I shuffled forward, feeling nothing. My gaze became caught in the endlessly elaborated pattern of frozen translucent explosions, tiny splayed hexagonal pillars thrown partly out by the ground and interwoven in concatenated series stretching from beneath my feet everywhere I looked. Whole crystal layers wide as fields had been forced up, tilting, grinding together until their contiguous edges shattered, forming a ridge crowned with awry crystals. The rings and interlocking curves of the pattern expanded about me, exploding slowly with a gleam as light linked them to my eye, reiterating their theme: six, six minus a spoke of its explosion or sharing one with its neighbor, a tiny brilliant sexagonal gleam from the tip of a crystal, six, six. Dust glittered where crystals had fought while growing. "See that dust, An," Dack said. "I'm surprised there's not more of it. Perhaps it recombines. You'll have noticed that the surface is relatively level. This is because the crystal growth is slow and even. So much so that if I hadn't been photographing this world regularly I wouldn't have observed it. This means that the conflicts of growth cause pulverization, so that any uplift or deformation is local and minor. But that brings us back to the dust." I supposed this might be his way of including me. But it occurred to me as his voice nagged against my ear that it had more to do with his need to possess a landscape. Not that it mattered. I didn't feel it, simply registered it intellectually.

"Chisel, Dack," Hebby said. I glanced over as Dack hobbled to him, and saw the dull gleam of omn. No doubt they'd chosen it for its hardness. Since I hadn't told them about Earth-7 and omn and me, I could hardly expect them to know. But all I felt was exclusion, from them and from the landscape.

I gazed at a nearby erect crystal. It was as creamily opaque as the ground underfoot, where several layers of crystal collaborated to reflect light and to make me feel attended by a constant mobile white stage. The shadow of the crystal was poised on the lip of a ridge; in a moment it would slip over. I waited, engrossed. Time attenuated. Perhaps the ridge was growing as the shadow moved and they would maintain equilibrium. No, the ridge was slower. I felt my mind adjusting to the pace of Eveningstar.

I felt a tugging at my mind. A blink of blinding light, searing my mind but gone before I felt it was more than a pure imperative. A light something like my mother. No, she was far back down my mind, and this was too violent and bright. I had to contain it, it threatened to burn, it was intolerable. I sketched an outline from its after-image and enclosed it next time it came. It was a woman. From her neck grew a featureless head of white crystal. It was me: Hebby's subliminal version of the Fecunds' fears. "An, I've been calling you for minutes," his voice said in my ear. "Is she moving? I think she's heard us at last."

"Sorry, I was thinking," I said, turning back to them resentfully when I saw that while I'd been distracted the shadow had made its move. They were both watching me through masks of reflected crystal.

I hung back when we returned to the planethopper, perhaps because I could at least explain my sense of unreality while outside and suited. When I entered at last and sealed the doors Hebby and Dack had their backs to me and were unscrewing their helmets. They reminded me of jars I'd opened when I was little to see what was inside. Suddenly I became fascinated. What was inside the helmets?

The helmets came off and I saw something strange and disturbing: the backs of two heads. I'd never looked at them before, these faceless featureless swellings covered with growth, one stubbly and dry gray, a bit patchy, the other fatter, sitting on pink rings of neck, its bulb heavy with hanging moist brown coils. Delicate pink protrusions with a thicker rim emerged on either side of the growth. Now the bulbs were moving around through the hollow cramped rectangle of space in the cabin, bobbing on their thick stalks. I removed my own helmet and suit and began to search the cabin for sixes, on which my mind could more easily fasten—a sexagonal accident of shadow on the floor, a chance arrangement of the instruments Dack was removing from storage. Eventually my gaze rested on the landscape outside.

Satisfied after a while, my mind explored the cabin again. The others had been examining and analyzing their crystals, pursuing them through magnifications, submitting them to the action of a chemical simulator. "No trace of a solvent. Certainly no metamorphic activity, there's no structural difference between the samples I can see," Hebby said, among other things I couldn't recall. "They're still growing but there's no expenditure of energy. It's like geological evolution speeded up but with no energy perceptible. A life of their own, almost," Dack said. "Notice that they tend to concavity. It's worth considering implosion as their motive force, an implosion immediately translated into growth." I let their voices drift through me, and watched while Dack trained a heatrod on a crystal, and the flesh beneath his chin glowed red then white, and the surface on which he was working darkened as it prepared to melt or to burst into flame. "Isn't that dangerous?" I said.

"Dack," Hebby said. "We don't want to be that sooner."

"She's doing it," Dack said; then with a strenuous simultaneously resented effort, "I don't mean I'm blaming you, An. Perhaps you're doing it unconsciously."

"Inefficiency's nobody's fault but your own," Hebby said.

"I'll be outside," I said.

"Don't be stupid. Dack, you finish now. We're all tired. I don't think I've ever felt so tired. It's the change in gravity. Eat now then sleep, and tomorrow we can finish and be far."

"You say sleep as if it were easy. It isn't for me," Dack said, primed with frustration.

"Then make the effort."

"I mean to go outside for a while," I said. "I need peace before I can be useful. I began to feel it out there before. I'll be half an hour and I don't intend to hurt myself. You'll be able to see me if you look."

"Stay near the hopper," Hebby said, and a smile in his eyes sought a reflection in mine. I didn't understand why; my own words had meant little to me, I'd simply wanted to attach the sixes that were floating restlessly in my mind to something. Then I realized: he thought I was leaving to give them an opportunity to rid themselves of tension. No doubt that was a good reason. I nodded. Dack watched us, frowning.

I was surprised to find how near the sun was to the horizon. As I descended the colours of the plain were switched on. They distracted me; they weren't sixes, and they blotted out everything else. In some way they reminded me of my mother. It occurred to me that I'd never felt anyone else's death. Of course there hadn't been anyone else close to me who could have died. But it was odd that I'd never even felt a hint of the numerous deaths that must have happened near me. I remembered realizing that I'd become partially blind as a telepath; this might have been where the blind spot had begun growing. Not that I'd felt my mother's death, rather the reverse; I'd felt continuity. Perhaps it wasn't my mother in my mind at all but only my idea of her. Her light began to flutter wildly deep in my mind, and I hastily directed my thoughts elsewhere.

I floated. Lights, one of them presumably my mother, hung around me. Above me were Hebby and Dack. Globed inside myself, I began to accumulate an impression which, now I let it gather, stretched back as far as an undefined moment in our approach to Eveningstar. Very approximately, it was an impression that my mind had been moving, perhaps rotating, from light to shadow then into light again. So vague was the notion that I couldn't begin to determine in which direction I was now moving, if it were a matter of my moving at all. I assumed there had to be a point at which the umbra reached maximum intensity. I didn't know how to work out whether I'd passed that point, or what happened when it was reached.

My mind felt as if having drifted free of all externals it were imploding. I disliked the sensation, and began to climb back toward the planethopper. But no doubt Hebby and Dack were pairing. At least I could hold myself stable by them. I stood clutching the rungs and entered Hebby and Dack.

They were pairing. I'd never seen men doing so, let alone shared the essence of it. But it confirmed the view of pairing I'd had for as long as I could remember: a rather clumsy rather absurd sort of physical and sometimes mental toil, which worked in proportion to how successfully you could blind yourself to its mechanics. Indeed, both of them were surprised and depressed by the amount of toil required this time.

Hebby was thinking of me outside, reassuring himself that I was safe, wishing he could pair with me both for his sake and mine, but reminding himself that he had to stay faithful to Dack, who needed that. I traced myself through his mind. Thanks, he was thinking, thanks that she didn't ask why the Home was so close to that corpsefield. Especially since it disturbed her and she must have realized how it upset Dack. Image: once a field was sufficiently fertile the Fecunds broke down another less fertile area and went there to die. Thanks that we managed to avoid telling her that. We'd have heard crop rotation and manuring and intelligence, and no flight to Eveningstar.

He was right, I thought. There'd been questions I should have realized needed to be asked. There was more to Fecundity than I'd known or they'd admitted. Maybe I could go back and have another look.

Dack was thinking about not thinking about Earth-6, which made it easy for me to slip through the lapses in his control. Learning geology on Earth-6, so far as it was taught. Another boy on the same course who agreed that everyone on Earth-6 was trying to live in a mirror. Sharing an apartment with him. Both getting narcoticized one night and pairing, a brief violent desperate image swept aside by Dack's mind but not before I'd examined it: the boy represented everything

Dack wanted to feel was true and pairing a gesture against everything false, a rather self-conscious equation I could neither decipher nor solve. Dack's mind was beginning to writhe, barriers sprang up to divert me into endless paths of disguising trivia. I knew he could lure me into the maze he'd built of himself. But drained of sympathy, I suddenly felt colossally powerful. I forged straight to the culmination of his disgust.

I was on the edge of one of the fields on Fecundity. Several dozen Fecunds were standing on fallen trees among the corpses. They were gazing in various directions, and all of them were absolutely still. Dack's mind was writhing frantically, and up in the planet-hopper his body was squirming to be free of the threat of memory, but I followed the image as it burrowed deeper into his unconscious. It was the emblem of all that was moist, of irrepressible frightful growth. The nearest Fecunds were gazing at a corpse a few yards from me. Its dry mound of skin was stubbled with grass, and beside it lay several burst yellow shells. As I watched a rent in the skin parted further and young glideworms began to emerge, a few at a time. Clouds of pastel colour drifted across their raised wings and instantly vanished as the wings dried. Then the glideworms rose in a fluttering mass, spread out and sped gliding into the jungle. The heads of the Fecunds rose to watch, and their still gazes followed the flight until it was obscured by the trees. Then Dack's mind shuddered violently, forcing his loathing up almost to the surface. Having learned everything I emerged.

As soon as they'd finished pairing I returned to the cabin. They looked hot, exhausted, flustered. Hebby realized at once what my timing implied. He wasn't sure whether I'd experienced their pairing as a purely impersonal sensation, without reference to them. He thought it had perhaps helped and included me a little. Dack's realization was more gradual, and I was already in my chair behind my closed eyes, shutting them out because their presence nagged at my ease, and thinking I would rather return to Fecundity than go with them.

When I awoke it was bright. The sun was almost overhead. Dack was using a microscope while Hebby gazed from the window and made calculations. Light hung around me, trapped into confusions by the surfaces of the cabin. I wondered for a moment why I could see only confusion, then realized that the instruments and controls weren't familiar to me, never had been. I closed my eyes.

My glimpses of the cabin expanded lethargically through my mind. They parted like treacle and sailed away, and six grew in my mind. I began to see and think six. I felt a gradual steady intensification. Of what? My mind was approaching a point of transition. I opened my eyes. Hebby and Dack were where I'd last seen them, it seemed a long time ago. They weren't six. But it did seem an enormously long time since I'd seen them. "Aren't we taking longer than we meant to?" I said at last.

Hebby stared at me as if he were having trouble focusing, he glared at the distraction. "No," he said in a tone meant to express the effort of speaking.

Some time later I heard him say beyond my closed eyelids: "The growth is accelerating. It has been since we landed if my calculations are correct. Not just the samples, the whole place. But there's still no energy to speak of being released. If there's danger it may be of a kind we wouldn't recognize. Dack, I'm talking to you."

I opened my eyes. Hebby was staring at Dack, who was trying to use his microscope at least a foot away from his eye. I felt Hebby's thought, directed consciously straight at me: if you can feel me thinking then try to feel what's happened to Dack. Then it was gone, doused by the knowledge that I couldn't tell him even if I discovered something, because that would destroy the vestiges of trust. What a game, I thought. Not worth playing.

Dack saw us both staring at him. "She's doing it," he shouted. "She's inside us all the time. If she isn't, ask her why she didn't want us to make ourselves clearer instead of just her. She betrayed herself there. She's in my mind and I can't get hold of it."

"I wish I could feel what's wrong with him," I said to Hebby. "But it's gone completely. I only felt you asking because you thought it straight at me. I think we're all being affected by the crystal somehow. We should leave while we can."

I don't think I could have persuaded them. But they both turned automatically and looked toward the control panels, and realized that they couldn't see them.

The knowledge was so sudden and shocking I even felt it for a moment. All they could see was a jumble of light and metal and synthetic, no sixes. While they had been analyzing the crystals their minds had been letting go of anything they weren't referring directly to.

And because they had been preoccupied I hadn't felt them going, or if I had I'd confused it with my own experience.

They were on the edge of shock. Hebby looked blinded. Dack's hands were moving restlessly and his thumbs were burrowing into his fists. I realized that I wouldn't be able to have another look at Fecundity. Not unless someone picked us up. "The distress signal," I said.

I felt their minds stirring and reaching tentatively into the chaos of surfaces and light before retreating baffled. I tried to remember the signal. Six. Half six. It had three legs. "It's red," I remembered suddenly. "Look for red."

Eventually they found it, clipped to a wall. I hadn't moved from my seat, because the doors were a little ahead on my left and I had an intuition that if I moved and lost the doors we would be completely disoriented. "You set it up, Dack," I said, because Hebby was hardly moving.

"Do as she says," Hebby said.

I watched Dack moving toward the doors. There was a discordant image in the middle distance of my mind, something about the inside of a balloon. Dack opened the inner door. "Close that," I said triumphantly. "Spacesuit first."

I felt his muffled resentment of the games that were being played with him. I managed to remember where I'd been standing when I'd last closed the balloon over my head, and pointed until my arm grew tired and they found the suits. "Bring me mine, Hebby," I said. "And get yours. If we all suit there'll be less chance of a mistake." I meant that we could watch

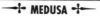

each other to avoid amnesiac mistakes in suiting but I probably sounded more callous. I was tiring of this game of using words.

We suited in a circle, watching each other fumble. It was like a play acted by cretins. I stood with part of me always touching my chair, to maintain orientation. At last we'd compared our suiting and agreed on the crucial elements we should have in common. Then I opened the inner door. Dack shuffled forward with the signal. "Switch it on," I said, and after some consultation we managed to activate the bulb and presumably its broadcast. I closed the door behind Dack.

An orange bulb lit. After a good deal of slow sticky thought I realized that this wasn't the distress signal but the indicator showing that the outer door had opened. My hand remained on the door controls. Some considerable time probably passed before I said to Hebby: "Let's stand in the door. There's just about room for us both. Then we can see if he needs help."

I managed to close the outer door and open the inner. I guided Hebby in. His mind had obviously collapsed into passivity. I followed him and reversed the opening of the doors.

The sun had almost reached the horizon. Beneath the dusting of pinpoints of light the sixes were reiterated endlessly, imperceptibly yet inexorably growing. I moved forward to stand pressed against Hebby at the top of the ladder. As we looked down our helmets scraped together. Perhaps they would shatter. My mind filled with six.

Then, as we traced the pattern back toward us, we saw Dack. He was standing over the distress signal, which had fallen on its side near the planethopper's jets. He was glaring down at it as if it were an intruder. His posture promised violence.

"No," Hebby said. It was a syllable of almost inarticulate agonized terror. He swung himself out onto the ladder and hurried down. I watched his hooded helmet jerk downward with a silent bump bump bump. Then the sixes stretched before me unobscured. Before I had quite absorbed them I remembered that if the signal weren't set up we wouldn't be able to see Fecundity again. I wasn't so sure now that I wanted to, but I felt it was my right. I grasped the holds and felt my way onto the ladder.

At the bottom I met what looked like a static hologram. Hebby had lost impetus and was standing just beyond the ladder. Dack hadn't moved. He looked engrossed in sixes now, and no doubt the presence of the signal had ceased to disturb him. Both of them were blurred by the hovering mist of multicoloured light suspended almost as far as the horizon.

As I came alongside him Hebby moved with me. Perhaps his renewed terror again gave him impetus, for he outdistanced me and had almost reached the signal before Dack saw him. I was slowing, for my mind and the inexorable rolling had almost attuned. No doubt the same was happening to Hebby and Dack, and perhaps the only instinct left to Dack was physical self-preservation. Perhaps, seeing us both bearing down on the signal, he thought we'd finally united against him. Whyever, he picked up the signal and with one of the legs smashed Hebby's helmet.

There was a crack and a brief high wheeze of breath. Hebby fell beneath the jets. The blow must have damaged his helmet transmitter, for it kept sputtering and buzzing against my ears. I continued walking. Dack backed away, raising the signal over his head, and fell backwards over Hebby. The signal fell near me, I think. It must have been the heavy object I picked up. Drifting images: red, no doubt that of the signal; a high sound (Hebby's broken transmitter?); raising the signal and letting it fall several times, no doubt to test its weight; flinging it as far as it would go.

I found my way back into the planethopper before my suit's air gave out. With a completely irrational notion of making for Fecundity I pulled at a few of the surfaces where I remembered the control panel to be. When some of them moved and a shudder passed through the planethopper I returned to myself a little and hurriedly shoved them back into place. I realized that some indeterminate time ago I'd passed the point where the graduating shadow achieved greatest intensity in my mind. I took off my spacesuit and all my clothes, whose insistent presence was beginning to annoy me, and sat in my chair.

Ahead the landscape was dark. But six was in my mind, implicit there so that I no longer had to search for it. After a long slow growth a concept formed in my mind. It hung there, slowly crystallizing until it had translated itself in terms of my mind. Thus: good. It was good. It was useful.

I was useful to think with. I had been added to a mind.

There were other concepts that my mind helped to form:

Unalterable six, increasing.

All becomes six.
Slowly rolling.
They took me several weeks.

V

Eventually there was sound, I was being moved, sixes were dimming as they were pulled away from me. There were pale pink bulbs around and above me with moist globes and wet slits moving, making sounds: faces. My mind began to attenuate as its supporting sixes retreated, it became too thin to support even its own weight, and much later I awoke on *Argosy-18*.

People came into the cabin to look at me and I lay looking at them. All of them looked in pain or worried, not necessarily by me. I observed that my time-sense was returning, although I could only assume that it was gradually approaching objectivity. Food was brought in, which I ate. Eventually one of the people who had been looking at me reappeared and introduced himself. He was Lun, a shipman telepath. ''I've been reading what happened from you,'' he said.

''I didn't feel you doing it.''

''That's part of what's still wrong.'' At the back of his eyes was a sad fear. ''If it helps, we've been able to deduce approximately what was happening,'' he said. ''That crystal's a unique phenomenon, far as we know. How it grows we can't tell, but the energy it releases is closer to thought than any other form we know. So your consciousness and those of your companions had to restructure themselves to comprehend the effect. That's our physicist's hypothesis. We want nothing to

86

do with the crystal, be sure. We might have it put out of orbit, though the bridge thinks that might upset the balance on Fecundity somehow."

I thought that might or might not be a pity. "Did I kill Dack?" I said.

"Yes, so far as I can tell. Your mind isn't clear on that point. It isn't traumatized, there's simply a perception which can't be translated without a restructuring you would have to achieve yourself. That's where the only evidence is. When you were trying to pilot the hopper you destroyed the bodies. Thank your clumsiness: you didn't put out the distress signal completely, only its broadcast. I've told the bridge that your companions made a suicide pact. Effect of the crystal. If the bridge can't trust their telepath they can't trust anyone."

"Then you don't blame me."

"Not for everything, no. At this stage blame isn't relevant. Cure is, and that's what I'm here to talk about." He halted until I sat up. "Recall what happens when a Fecund is wounded. When we couldn't make contact with the Fecundity Home a party went down. Among them was our visitors welcome officer, new this trip. He turned out to be a latent xenophobe. It was deep, because they hadn't discovered it on his own ship, even our selection panel hadn't. Nor me, too busy cradling our visitors. He shot three Fecunds. They aren't dead, and our doctor who luckily is as nonsensitive a man as you could meet is healing them now. But it's been bad. Recall how people have looked. We're completing our parabola now to pick him up, and it's getting worse."

"I can't feel it," I said.

"Exactly." His eyes repeated the sense of each phrase. "That's why I think you could survive if you went down to Fecundity now. Survive in one sense, that is. To survive completely you would have to feel their cry. Your loss of feeling has saved you so far, but you have to be a telepath or nothing. I've seen someone go telepathically blind, and be sure it's death, inevitable passive suicide. Now this could damage you, or it could be gradual enough for you to bear. But there's a draw in you toward Fecundity. And that intuition is all you have left."

There was more to see on Fecundity, fewer people, I thought: that was something. "All right," I said.

"The boat that picks up the doctor will take you down. I've persuaded the bridge that you're capable of withstanding the cry until it's over and incapable of doing harm. That at least will be true, because we're having all potential weapons removed from the Home. No knives, no breakable containers. You'll have to subsist on dehydrates and local edibles, I'm afraid. We've put out a personnel call but you'll be alone until the next *Argosy* docks, maybe longer. And once you're there, even if you want to it may be a long time before you can leave."

I wished he would be quiet. I was sure the Fecunds' cries couldn't be more nagging. "I've said all right," I said.

As the boat sank toward Fecundity I felt nothing. I gazed up at the two hundred yards of the *Argosy*, like a white horizontally hanging drop with its point truncated, reeling out the boat on threads of remote control. I gazed down at the Home rising on its stage of dust,

and the doctor standing near the white pillar, among carriers full of potential weapons.

When he'd gone I entered the Home. I ate a dehydrate and drank some Fecundity wine. I looked into my room. One carrier full of lesser personals still hung on a branch. The personals I'd taken with me in the planethopper I had left on *Argosy-18* for whoever wanted them.

I began to walk through the six levels of crescented rooms and trunks and hammocks. When I tired of that I went into Hebby's and Dack's room. I was surprised how little they'd left: a few carved roots, a diary with Dack's signature but no entries. There was a faint lightening deep in my mind. It annoyed me because I couldn't define what it was.

After some hours I'd exhausted sitting in the Home. It vexed me to have to put on a snapsuit, but I supposed there wasn't much point in suffering from exposure. Besides, it vexed me more to sit brooding on the dimly waxing not quite definable light in my mind, which throbbed dully like the first prolonged threat of toothache. I went toward the jungle.

The colours were fading slightly as evening approached. Still, I found their profusion intolerable; they were too varied and distracting, they wouldn't leave me alone. I entered the main path toward the field, walking because I knew to return to the Home would allow me no relief. The light insisted, flickering almost into coherence. What was it like?

Ahead of me several Fecunds were returning two abreast from the field, and at once my mind produced a memory and seized it. The light was my mother. I could feel her now, fluttering nervously and frantically in the midst of a great cold hollow, fluttering in terror of the hollow that knew her only as a nagging light, in terror of total annihilation. I know I'm the hollow, I said into myself. But I can't feel yet, and it may get worse. I've carried you so as to release you. This is the best place we've been. I'm going to release you here. There may not be anywhere better.

The light began to tremble and my mind moved to close protectively about it, surrounding it with memories. I tried to recapture my feelings when I'd held my mother's continuity in my mind. I couldn't, but I grasped the memory as hard as I could. Then, thrusting with all of me, I let go.

There was a scream, a tearing, a sensation as if there were a raw jagged hole full of nerve-ends somewhere in me. It throbbed, it wept. The scream stopped, because I'd closed my mouth. Because I was looking at the Fecunds, which had halted and were gazing at me. Apart from in Dack's memory, I'd never seen them so still.

Through the hole I'd gouged in myself slowly trickled, then flowed, then flooded the cry of the wounded Fecunds. That, and more. Carried with it and intensifying, so that I felt as if it were addressed directly to me, was a planetful of wordless soothing.

It was dark when I groped my way onto the clearing around the Home. I'd been sick, my limbs were shaking, I was so weak I made no distinction between walking and crawling. Around me the Fecunds were covered. I let my body make its way toward the Home and gazed inside myself.

Within my mind was an area like a bright cold ray,

which couldn't feel the Fecunds. It widened toward my memories of Eveningstar and dwindled toward the further past. Outside it, like a penumbra of colour, was my sense of the Fecunds.

I lay in my hammock. Somewhere within the blinded ray were the deaths of Hebby and Dack. Their continuity was there if anywhere. If I could retrieve their essences they might not be so dead. Perhaps Fecundity would give me my memories, or perhaps I would have to make the journey alone. Either way, delusion would be ready for me. I slept, and then I waited. And wait.

† RISING GENERATION †

As they approached the cave beneath the castle some of the children began to play at zombies, hobbling stiffly, arms outstretched. Heather Fry frowned. If they knew the stories about the place, despite her efforts to make sure they didn't, she hoped they wouldn't frighten the others. She hadn't wanted to come at all; it had been Miss Sharp's idea, and she'd been teaching decades longer than Heather, so of course she had her way. The children were still plodding inexorably toward their victims. Then Joanne said ''You're only being like those men in that film last night.'' Heather smiled with relief. ''Keep together and wait for me,'' she called.

She glanced up at the castle, set atop the hill like a

crown, snapped and bent and discolored by time. Over-head sailed a pale blue sky, only a wake of thin foamy clouds on the horizon betraying any movement. Against the sky, just below the castle, Heather saw three figures toiling upward. Odd, she thought, the school had been told the castle was forbidden to visi-tors because of the danger of falling stone, which was why they'd had to make do with the cave. Still, she was glad she hadn't had to coax her class all the way up there. The three were moving slowly and clumsily, no doubt exhausted by their climb, and even from where Heather stood their faces looked exceptionally pale.

She had to knock several times on the door of the guide's hut before he emerged. Looking in beyond him, Heather wondered what had taken his time. Not tidying the hut, certainly, because the desk looked blitzed, scattered and overflowing with forms and even an upset ink-bottle, fortunately stoppered. She looked at the guide and her opinion sank further. Clearly he didn't believe in shaving or cutting his nails, and he was pale enough to have been born in a cave, she thought. He didn't even bother to turn to her; he stared at the children lined up at the cave entrance, though by his lack of expression he might as well have been blind. "I'd rather you didn't say anything about the legend," she said.

His stare swivelled to her and held for so long she felt it making a fool of her. "You know what I mean," she said, determined to show him she did too. "The stories about the castle. About how the baron was supposed to keep zombies in the cave to work for him, until some-one killed him and walled them up. I know it's only a story, but not for the children, please."

When he'd finished staring at her he walked toward the cave, his hands dangling on his long arms and almost brushing his knees. At least he won't interrupt, she thought. I wonder how much he's paid, and for what? There was even a propped-up boot poking out from beneath the desk.

As she reached the near end of the line of children he was trudging into the cave. Daylight slipped from his back and he merged with the enormous darkness, then the walls closed about him as his torch awakened them. Heather switched on her own torch. "Stay with your partner," she called, paragraphing with her fingers. "Stay in the light. And don't lag."

The children, fourteen pairs of them, were hurrying after the guide's light. The cave was wide at the entrance but swiftly narrowed as it curved, and when Heather glanced back a minute later, lips of darkness had closed behind them. As the guide's torch wavered the corrugations of the walls rippled like the soft gulping flesh of a throat. The children were glancing about uneasily like young wild animals, worried by the dark sly shifting they glimpsed at the edge of their vision. Heather steadied her beam about them, and the thousands of tons of stone above their heads closed down.

Not that it was easy to steady the beam. In the cave he'd picked up speed considerably, and she and the children had to hurry so as not to be left behind. Maybe he feels at home, she thought angrily. "Will you slow down, please," she called, and heard Debbie at the front of the line say, "Miss Fry says you've got to slow down."

The guide's light caught a wide flat slab of roof that

looked as if it were sagging. Scattered earth crunched softly beneath Heather's feet. About now, she was sure, they would be heading up and out the other side of the hill. Joanne, who hadn't let Debbie convince her as a zombie, and Debbie squeezed back to Heather along the contracting passage. "I don't like that man," Joanne said. "He's dirty."

"What do you mean?" Heather said, sounding too worried.

But Joanne said, "He's got earth in his ears."

"Will you hold our hands if we're frightened?" Debbie said.

"Now I can't hold everyone's hand, can I?" Earth slid from beneath Heather's feet. Odd, she thought: must come from the guide's ears and beneath his nails, and began to giggle, shaking her head when they asked why. He was still forcing them to hurry, but she was beginning to be glad that at least they wouldn't have to depend on him much longer. "If you think of questions don't ask them yet," she called. "Wait until we're outside."

"I wish we didn't have to come underground," Joanne said.

Then you should have said before, Heather thought. "You'll be able to look for things in the field later," she said. And at least you haven't had Miss Sharp herding you as well as her own class. If they hadn't come on ahead they would have had to suffer her running their picnic.

"But why do we have to come down when it's nice? Sharon didn't have to."

"It'll be nice this afternoon. Sharon can't go into

places that are closed in, just as you don't like high places. So you see, you're lucky today."

"I don't feel lucky," Joanne said.

The ridges of the walls were still swaying gently, like the leaves of a submarine plant, and now one reached out and tugged at Heather's sleeve. She flinched away then saw that it was a splintered plank, several of which were propped against the wall, looking as if they'd once been fastened together. Ahead the cave forked, and the children were following the shrinking rim of light into the left-hand passage, which was so low that they had to stoop. "Go on, you're all right," she told Debbie, who was hesitating. Stupid man, she raged.

It was tighter than she'd thought. She had to hold one arm straight out in front of her so that the light urged the children on, leaving herself surrounded by darkness that coldly pressed her shoulders down when she tried to see ahead. If this passage had been fenced off, as she suspected, she was sorry it had been re-opened. The children's ridged shadows rippled like caterpillars. Suddenly Debbie halted. "There's someone else in here," she said.

"Well?" Joanne said. "It's not your cave."

Now all the children had gone quiet, and Heather could hear it too: the footsteps of several people tramping forward from deeper within the cave. Each step was followed by a scattering sound like brief dry rain. "Men working in the caves," she called, waiting for someone to ask what the dry sound was so that she could say they were carrying earth. Don't ask why, she thought. Something to do with the castle, perhaps with the men she'd seen on the hill. But the footsteps had stopped.

When she straightened up at last the darkness clenched on her head; she had to steady herself against the wall. Her vertigo gradually steadied, and she peered ahead. The children had caught up with the guide, who was silhouetted against a gaping tunnel of bright pale stone. As she started toward him he pulled something from his pocket and hurled it beyond her.

Debbie made to retrieve it. "It's all right," Heather said, and ushered the pair of them with her light toward the other children. Then, cursing his rudeness, she turned the beam on what she assumed he'd thrown her to catch. She peered closer, but it was exactly what it seemed: a packed lump of earth. Right, she thought, if I can lose you your job, you're out of work now.

She advanced on him. He was standing in the mouth of a side tunnel, staring back at her and pointing his torch deeper into the main passage. The children were hurrying past him into the hard tube of light. She was nearly upon him when he plodded out of the side tunnel, and she saw that the children were heading for a jagged opening at the limit of the beam, surrounded by exploded stone sprinkled with earth. She'd opened her mouth to call them back when his hand gripped her face and crushed her lips, forcing her back into the side tunnel.

His cold hand smelled thickly of earth. His arm was so long that her nails flailed inches short of his face. "Where's Miss Fry?" Debbie called, and he pointed ahead with his torch. Then he pushed Heather further into the cave, though she hacked at his shins. All at once she remembered that the boot beneath the desk had been propped on its toe: there might have been a leg beyond it.

Then the children screamed; one chorus of panic, then silence. Heather's teeth closed in the flesh of his hand, but he continued to shove her back into the cave. She saw her torch gazing up at the roof of the main passage, retreating. His own torch drooped in his hand, and its light drew the walls to leap and struggle, imitating her.

Now he was forcing her toward the cave floor. She caught sight of a mound of earth into which he began to press her head, as if for baptism. She fought upward, teeth grinding in his flesh, and saw figures groping past her upturned torch. They were the children.

She let herself go limp at once, and managed to twist out of the way as he fell. But he kept hold of her until she succeeded in bringing her foot forward and grinding his face beneath her heel like a great pale insect. He still made no vocal sound. Then she fled staggering to her torch, grabbed it, and ran. The stone wrinkles of the low roof seemed more hindering, as if now she were battling a current. Before she was free of the roof she heard him crawling in the darkness at her heels, like a worm.

When the children appeared at the end of her swaying tunnel of light she gave a wordless cry of relief. She could feel nothing but relief that they were covered with dirt: they'd been playing. They still were, just short of the border of daylight, and they'd even persuaded Joanne to be a zombie. "Quickly," Heather gasped. "Run to Miss Sharp's class." But they con-

tinued playing, turning stiffly toward her, arms groping. Then, as she saw the earth trickling from their
mouths and noses, she knew they weren't playing
at all.

† RUN THROUGH †

The figure was there again. Glancing up the hill as he searched for the key, Blair could just make it out framed in one of the cottage's small window-panes, a figure standing at the edge of the trees. Never mind, he ordered himself, looking beneath the table for the key. Never mind the key, he snarled, I'm here to write a story, I should be trying to retrieve the plot. But he'd been doing so all day, without success. That was why he had walked up the hill.

He'd been tramping back and forth through the cottage all morning, now and then forcing himself to sit at the table and scribble a page which he would type and at once crumple up. Eventually, feeling as if the low beams were resting all their weight on his head, he went outside. Fields of grass dazzled him, pressing perspectiveless against his eyes. The hint of a breeze touched him, the line of trees on the horizon moved uneasily in their sleep. He began to walk.

Even then he might not have walked up the hill if he hadn't remembered what the landlord of the cottage had said: "Are you fond of trees?" "No, not especially," Blair had admitted. "When I'm writing a book I don't notice much outside it." "Ah, well," and the landlord had clearly been stumbling, "I was only going to say there's a forest half a mile away that's worth seeing." Rather than that senile clump up the hill, Blair had thought, walking. Why would he have bothered to divert me from going up there? Let's go and see.

Perhaps because it was blighted, he'd thought five minutes later. The branches of the oaks which encircled the hill about halfway up were thickly intertwined overhead like tangled antlers; the tops of the trunks looked crumpled, malformed. The bark was split and peeling, and beneath it squirmed white glistening grubs. Ah, rural charm, Blair thought. Nevertheless he'd slipped gingerly between the trees. There had to be more to the wood, surely.

No, the key won't be in those drawers, I've never opened them, he thought, remembering distractedly that darkness had settled over him, and dimness. The next highest ring of oaks stretched its branches toward the first, squeezing out all but trickles of daylight, which lay stranded on the muddy grass. Blair had felt cut off from the summer day, penned in with the dim moist stillness. When he'd looked back the spaces between the outer trees were shrunken, darkening even the glimpses of bright fields beyond. He'd pushed between the slippery trunks of the inner ring, wondering why so carefully grown a wood should have been neglected. There must be a story here.

He'd found himself almost at the crown of the hill. Above him stood an ingrown clump of oaks, their dank-leaved branches resting on one another's trunks like the wings of gossiping bats. The cramped glade seemed as dim as the bottom of a muddy pool. He'd turned, trying to use the sunlight beyond the rings of trees. Gradually his eyes had grasped the light, coaxing details from within silhouettes. And suddenly he'd seen a face staring at him from a trunk.

He'd managed not to cry out during the moments it took him to see what it was: a hollow-eyed face carved from the trees. Great square stern faces thrust forward from the wood of all the trees that made up the inner ring. It was as if the trees still stood guard, though dead. Stood guard on what? Let's see, quickly. This wasn't helping his story.

The key isn't up the hill, he thought angrily, forcing his gaze away from the window, searching. As he'd moved toward the trees at the top of the hill a breeze had shuddered through the glade. As he'd turned toward the sound he'd glimpsed an eye opening in one of the faces. Urging himself closer, he'd seen that it was a bird within a hollow socket—but the bird hadn't moved as he approached. It was decomposed, almost indistinguishable from the splinters that transfixed it.

He'd made himself go back up to the central huddle of trees. When he'd managed to wrench apart some of the lower branches he had been both relieved and disappointed. Beneath the creaking canopy of branches was a pit, too dark for him to see within.

He'd stood there for minutes, giving his eyes time to adjust, but still he could see nothing except darkness. Cold air seemed to weigh him down like gathering ice. He'd leaned forward into the pit, peering intently, leaning on branches which creaked and suddenly gave way. The open throat of the pit had gaped beneath him. As he'd thrown himself back he had heard, deep in the pit, a bubbling sound like someone chuckling with a mouthful of mud, growing louder or rising toward him.

Then there had been hysterical confusion: battering his way out of the wood and running down the hill, heat clinging to his back, the blue sky cupped oppressively about him; then, for no reason he could grasp, desperately searching the cottage for the key to the outside door. As he was still doing, until he checked himself furiously. He didn't need the key to lock the door from the inside. Why had he begun searching?

If he'd known to begin with, the memory was confused now with the other bewilderments of the day. He had been ranging about the small low rooms when he'd noticed that one of the trees up the hill looked like a figure poised to rush toward him. He'd shrugged off the impression. Enough distractions. The key, for God's sake, the key.

When he'd grown so exhausted he found himself dashing from room to room for no reason at all, his brain feeling crushed and senseless, he made himself stop. What was he looking for? The key. Why? Even then, apparently, he hadn't known. I can see why the landlord tried to steer me away from that wood, he'd thought. Did my mind no good at all. He glanced through the window at the hill, and shrank back.

103

As soon as he'd looked at the hill a figure had left the trees and come speeding toward him, so fast that he'd taken seconds to react and then had flinched away, as if from a missile. He looked again. There was nothing except the dead wood, trembling with heat-haze. The haze must have conjured up the figure. The key. Must find the key. I'll need it. When I have to go out, that's when.

The sky had grown sullen, thunderous, an unbroken gray slab. Blair had stared at his manuscript on the table. The key can't be under there. Must get back to writing. First find the key.

The trees on the hill had caught a last lurid glare of sunlight before they sank back into the dullness. The figure had sprung forward from the smudged mass and hurtled toward Blair. There was no haze now. For God's sake let's see what it is. But his gaze had already flinched away, and when he'd glanced back there was no figure. It's this dim light, he'd thought. Just find the key. It'll ease my mind. I'm going round and round. I can't get at my story.

And he was still looped up in the distractions of his memory. The overcast had merged with twilight now; darkness gathered like unventilated smoke beneath the low beams. Blair made to switch on the light to help him search for the key. I don't need the key. Leave the light off and let's see what this is up the hill.

He gazed through the tiny pane. The hill formed slowly from the twilight, the trees were gouges of deeper darkness upon it. The place where he'd seemed to see the figure was at the opening closest to him in the outer ring of trees: there. And there it was, hurtling out of the twilight at him, rushing down the hill at a speed that clutched him helpless. The key, his mind cried, dragging him away from the window, the key!

Suddenly he realized that every time he had been on the point of seeing the figure as more than an approaching blur, his mind had recoiled, urging him away on any pretext it could find. Not this time, he thought, forcing it back by the scruff of his neck. Maybe if I get to the end of this story I can get on with writing my own.

Slowly his gaze again took hold of the dim forms on the hill. The figure had to wait until he could see it, he realized intuitively. Now he could, and now it was dashing down the hill at him, swelling up in his gaze as terror grew in his mind, as if the figure were a juggernaut that would crush him utterly. But he held his agonized gaze unwavering, and almost at the last moment the figure turned aside. He glimpsed its head, like a bulb squeezed white by fear. Then it was at the outside door.

The door didn't move, but Blair knew that the figure was scrabbling at the handle. It can't get in, he thought numbly. It hasn't got the key. And then he knew.

Even when it came to the window, thudding its hands against the tiny panes, he struggled not to be sure. Its face was pressed against the panes like white putty, leaving smears of panic. It slid snail-like across the panes, searching for the catch inside the window, trying with its thumping hands to break a pane to reach it. Though the face was squashed out of shape he could see it all too clearly. It was his own.

He tried to scream, but already he was outside, scrabbling in his pockets for the key, tearing at the grass and clods of earth for a rock to break the pane. It was hours ago again, and too late. Behind him he could hear the huge unhurried tread and bubbling chuckle that had followed him from the hill.

† WRAPPED UP †

As they neared the camp the archaeologist began to sing. Twill started violently and tried to hush him, but Long shook his head. The rheumatic groaning of their jeep on the cliff road must already have woken the camp. "That's your tent, isn't it?" Long demanded loudly of the archaeologist. "Over there, by the tomb?"

"There's my tent," the man said, pointing amid the camp; then, as he began to doze as if the effort of squinting had exhausted him, he added, "We're just passing the tomb."

Driving, Drabney smiled at Long's cleverness. Now they knew exactly where to go. The swaying headlights fastened on the tents and coaxed from the darkness behind them the outlines of palms like split and splintered poles. He made to switch off the lights, but restrained himself; it would look suspicious.

They were helping the archaeologist out of the jeep when a shadow rose up stiffly in one of the tents, like a joke-shop mummy. "All right," the archaeologist shouted, without slurring. "It's only me and some friends in need." They half-carried him to his tent, where he commenced singing at the darkness and offering it a drink. Then they hurried back to the jeep, whose motor was still running.

As they passed the place where he'd said the tomb was, Long and Twill jumped from the vehicle, clutching the sacks on which they'd been sitting. At once Drabney accelerated and drove loudly away, grinning. He couldn't believe it was going to be so easy.

When they'd seen the archaeologist in Cairo they had been dumbfounded by their luck. They had been sitting in a sidewalk café, so downcast they were almost prepared to drink. They'd had to flee Britain and America, where their faces were known. That had infuriated Drabney. All right, so they took wealth from people who were gullible enough to part with it. But it was because the people were susceptible to alcohol or other drugs that they left themselves so open. They were the ones to blame. The three had decided that a long time ago.

They'd heard that Cairo was full of drugs, but none of the susceptible people had seemed worth the effort. Then Twill, gazing dully on the packed dusty street, had recognized the archaeologist. The man whose last expedition had almost been ruined by his alcoholism! Who could only be here on another dig!

Twill knew something of archaeology, and it had

taken only half a bottle to pry loose the location of the dig, and the other half to make the man forget he'd told Twill. Then they'd merely had to camp nearby before the archaeologist and his party arrived, to become known locally as geologists on their own expedition, and to greet the archaeologist eventually as someone he vaguely remembered. "What a coincidence!" Twill had exclaimed. But even they hadn't expected their second encounter to coincide with the day the dig reached the tomb itself.

Once he was out of earshot of the camp Drabney parked the jeep and began to walk back, carrying his sack, checking his path intermittently with his torch. It had sounded as if the archaeologist was even going to leave his tomb open for them, the fool. "We aren't worried about the workers pilfering," he'd said. "I told them the mummies were those of magicians."

"That was clever," Twill had said.

"True, as well. The people who made this tomb for themselves blasphemed the whole Egyptian concept of life after death." Then he'd drifted off, muttering about tomb-robbers not daring to touch this tomb.

That's natives for you, Drabney thought as he walked. Gullible. Believed us when we said we were geologists. Full of drugs, probably, all of them. The rough cliff-top bit bluntly into his soles through his shoes. He reached the place where the tomb should be, and blinked his torch down the dark cliff at a faint glow. In a moment the torch-beams turned outward from the tomb twenty feet below and winked slyly at him.

They lit the stepped path while he clambered down. Then, as he entered the mouth, the beams swung about and gouged a rough narrow passage of tawny lime-stone brightly from the blackness. Rubble gnashed underfoot.

"Whoever they were, they must have impressed the people of their day," Twill whispered. "Notice there are no false doors, no pitfalls. They were sure nobody would dare to venture in. Still, it must have been easy enough to frighten people then."

Thirty feet into the cliff a stone door stood ajar. "We managed to move it a little," Long said. "They must have closed it again in case the air harmed anything."

Dust billowed thinly about them as they strained at the door with crowbars. Dust swarmed in the bowls of light balanced on the upturned torches planted on the rock floor. As the three heaved at the stone, chafing themselves against rock and against each other, their tethered shadows struggled overhead, bloating as if air were being squeezed up into them. When the door gave, a suddenly blacker shadow engulfed Drabney's. They inched out from behind the partly open door, then Drabney probed the gap with his torch.

He was expecting walls crowded with bright figures, the looming luster of golden coffins. Instead, his abashed torch revealed only rough limestone coffins with cracked lids, eight in all. The walls, when he turned to them, were muddily plastered but otherwise almost bare. In the corners, or what passed for such in the crudely-hollowed room, stood dark vague shapes like half-opened buds. Drabney wavered, disappointed and bewildered. It seemed less like a tomb than a cave-lair.

"He did say they didn't believe in possessions," Twill said anxiously.

"If you'd been him," Long retorted, "what would you have said? He wasn't that drunk."

Drabney realized why he'd thought of a lair. The hot, unpleasantly musty air which hung in the tomb reminded him of a zoo. The air, and something else. There was a faint creaking rustle in the depths of the room, beyond the dim edge of the light, as of something crawling torpidly in its lair.

"Go on," Twill said impatiently, and pushed him into the tomb. The light of his torch staggered forward as he did. The figure standing in the darkness, against the furthest wall, seemed to step forward jerkily to meet the light. It creaked softly, like leather.

Drabney felt as if a pitfall had opened in his stomach. Only the others, pressing close behind him, prevented his instinctive flight. When his torch-hand steadied, when the figure's wrappings of shadow had ceased to flap and writhe, the three stepped forward between the two ranks of coffins to see what was standing there.

It was a mummy, featureless and brown with wrappings. Yet somehow it was unlike the mummies Drabney had seen. The wrappings looked less like bandage than thick dry skin. He was sure he'd seen something like them before. The entire tall body creaked. As Drabney bent closer and the erased face peered blindly above him, he saw that the wrappings were minutely but perceptibly shifting, as if filling out.

"That's the change in temperature," Long said. "Come on. He's no use to us."

But Twill had stooped to pick up an object near the mummy's feet. It was a gilded sceptre two feet long, surmounted by a stylized pair of spread wings. "This

111

is a symbol of power," Twill said. "A high priest's, I'm sure it is. Why's a high priest standing there?"

"Maybe he put them all to bed and then couldn't tuck himself up."

"Come on, come on," Long said. "Time enough to joke when we're out of it."

Drabney hadn't intended his remark entirely as a joke. He watched Twill wrap the sceptre and put it in one of the sacks. Now it looked as if Drabney were playing the fool instead of filling his sack. Just because he didn't twitch like Twill didn't mean he couldn't equal him.

He shone his torch on a coffin and began to prize the lid apart along the crack. The lid was lighter than he'd expected; it parted easily, and the halves smashed on the floor. Drabney froze, trying to hold the silence still, as the others glared in speechless disgust. At last, when he was sure nobody at the camp had woken, he dared to move. He sank his light into the dustily fuming coffin.

The mummy within was clasped in wings of gold. The golden case which contained the body was almost featureless. The golden head was round and entirely blank, the feet were merged into a tapering tail. The rest of the case embraced itself with two enormous ribbed wings. Otherwise the coffin was empty. Shadows stirred the ribs of the wings as Drabney's torch moved.

"This one's the same," Long said when Drabney told him what he'd found. "The bastard, he was telling the truth. They weren't interested in anything but their religion. Look there."

He jabbed his light at the walls. In the center of each,

faded and crumbling now, a stylized series was painted: a man, a mummy, a winged figure poised to fly. "And there," Long said, snatching the shapes in the corners forward with his light. They were carved stone wings, about to open and reveal their ill-defined bodies.

"Maybe this is where the idea of angels came from," Drabney said.

"No need for that kind of talk," Twill said.

"No need for you to shout just because you can't find anything. What's wrong, is your friend there upsetting you?"

The mummy behind Twill was still creaking, with a sound like the stealthy flexing of disused leathery muscles. "Yes, it is," Twill said harshly. "How long is it going to make that row?"

He strode challengingly to the figure and thrust his torch at it. "Sometimes you act as if you need a shot yourself," Drabney said.

As Twill whirled furiously, brandishing a huge vague club of light, the end of his torch caught the mummy's neck. There was a sound of tearing.

All three lights seized the figure, like nooses. A long ragged strip of wrapping hung down its chest; the head, with its rudimentary face, was tilted askew. With a rush of horror, unable to bear the grotesque parody of what might lie beneath, Twill began to rip the wrappings from the mummy. Before Long could restrain him he had uncovered the head.

Perhaps they'd tried to make it look taller than it was. Or perhaps it hadn't been wrapped properly, and had partially decayed. Whatever the cause, the bald yellowed head within was barely half the size of its wrappings. It must be decay, Drabney thought, because the face looked sucked into itself, its features half-absorbed into the skull. Their lights wavered over the face, disturbing its shadows.

The face was moving. It wasn't the shadows at all. The head was shrinking, the eyes were collapsing into the skull. The head withdrew into the shoulders of the wrappings, and as it sank it fell back for a moment, as if with a soundless jagged-tooth laugh. It was the exposure to air, Drabney thought, the mummy was hurriedly decaying. Yet he felt uneasily that it was less like decay than like something else he'd once seen.

"I don't know what that achieved," Long said, hurrying through a capering of shadows to the door. "Come on, let's get these sacks filled and go."

"How?" Twill demanded shakily.

"Like this, since we have to." Long had removed the lid from the coffin nearest the door; now he plunged in a crowbar and began to wrench free pieces of the golden mummy-case. Twill recoiled, but Long said "We've no time to be delicate now. We want to be finished and out." Drabney hurried to help him, looking away as he shook out the contents, which the crowbar had crushed and broken.

From the back of the tomb came a large incessant rustling. Drabney imagined the figure collapsing entirely within its wrappings. Sweat crawled on him; the inert air pressed close. All three men fastened their lights determinedly on the coffin and the sacks.

They glanced toward the camp as they emerged, but it was dark and silent. They forced themselves to walk slowly, so as to hush their rattling sacks. Ahead was an inkling of dawn which had yet to touch the rock underfoot. At least, Drabney thought, they weren't so loaded that he would have to risk driving the jeep back to the others. He walked automatically, musing. Now he was out of the tomb he wanted to remember what he'd almost recognized in there.

He was still pondering when he heard the sound on his left, away from the cliff-edge: a faint creaking rustle. He peered, but sky and rocks had seeped together. Twill had heard it too, and started, jangling his sack. "Palms," Long explained. "That's all, for God's sake." But they could feel no wind. They began to hurry, heedless of the loud sacks at this distance from the camp.

Drabney struggled to unlock his mind. The dry leathery case of the mummy, the way its head had writhed and shrunk within—these were the things he recognized. But from where? He strode faster, shaking his head violently to dislodge a dark blot which it carried at the edge of his eye, seeming to pace him where sky and rock were dimly separating.

When he heard the creaking again he was sure it came from beyond the cliff-edge, from the void, moving leisurely with them. It was an acoustic effect, Drabney thought, an effect of the air which was congealing hotly about him as if it had clung to him from the tomb. That was all. For God's sake, he was fighting panic as if he were drugged. And all because of something he couldn't even remember, buried deep in his mind.

A dim form stood ahead, against the hint of dawn. It was not a rock. It was the jeep. "There was something not right about that tomb," Twill chattered, relieved, panting. "Those mummy-cases. Mummy-cases were a kind of sympathetic magic, you know. They were made to represent what you hoped to be after death."

"That wasn't what struck me as wrong," Long wheezed. "I'll tell you what I want to know. If that mummy standing against the wall really did attend to all the others, then who wrapped him?"

Suddenly Drabney remembered what he'd forgotten, and his heart began to thump him, urging him faster, faster. He ran, the treasure in his sack scraping harshly together. Somewhere, beyond the vast perspectiveless gray that hung close to his eyes, he heard a slow rhythmic creak and rustling, not at all like the sound of palm-trees. It was drawing swiftly nearer.

"Come on!" Drabney shouted wildly, grabbing at the jeep, bruising himself cruelly as he struggled in, cursing the ignition key as it squirmed out of reach in his pocket, cursing the others as they fumbled into the jeep. He could see nothing but the memory that had jarred loose at last, of what he'd once seen that had been like the mummy: a chrysalis, writhing in the throes of its final transformation.

He was still scrabbling at the ignition when the shrunken glaring wide-mouthed head pressed itself against the windscreen, smearing the glass as it clambered over and enfolded them all beneath its wings.

† PASSING PHASE †

When he realized where the song was coming
from Cox felt all the more confused.

Today he'd begun listening as soon as the children
reached the playground. He'd heard it once, but had
still been peering among the cramped games of foot-
ball, the leapfrogging little girls, the boys grunting
kung-fu style, when it ceased. The second time he was
ready; he hurried across the playground as stealthily as
he could—which was hardly at all, for most of the
children's faces turned up to him at once, steaming
with December breath. "Sign my autograph book, Mr.
Cox," someone pleaded. "I will later, Debbie," he
said, holding her small hand in his until she fell
behind.

He had to find the song. The more he heard it, the more he had to find out what it was. He'd thought it was a child's voice, but the closer he came—almost there now, quick—the less he thought so. The lilting treble was too pure; it was none of the voices he'd heard singing carols at assembly. And the song itself, the winding stream of obscurely harmonic melody, wasn't at all like the vocal doodling of an unselfconscious child. It meant something.

It was there, behind the young Bruce Lees. He pushed between them, risking threatened instant death. The song streamed on. It was coming from one of his class, Olivia, as she leaned against the wall. She was taking it out of her pocket. The song ceased, unfinished. But Cox had seen where it came from.

He stared at it, disappointed, bewildered. It was simply one of the coloured balls he'd seen some of the children carrying recently.

Not that these toys weren't themselves fascinating. He gazed at it, and so did Olivia, not even bothering to notice him. It was about an inch in diameter, fashioned smoothly of plastic or something equally light— Olivia handled it as if it weighed nothing at all. It spilled colours.

A kind of kids' psychedelic, he thought: harmless enough. The ball must be somehow prismatic, though he couldn't understand why it was more luminous than the surrounding light. Colours welled up, washing over the surface of the ball, colliding silently and recoiling, thrust apart by new colours. As they flooded over the ball and broke, Cox was momentarily sure he had never seen some of the colours before, as if the ball were helping him dream them.

Though he was engrossed he felt oddly detached. Perhaps he needed to hold the ball to be wholly engrossed. It was a bubble of green which burst at once, releasing blue, mauve, lemon, something else his mind snatched at vainly. He shook himself. "What's that called?" he asked Olivia.

"It's a ball." Surprisingly, she answered at once. She was one of his slower children, though appealingly protective. She wanted to be a vet. "It's only a toy," she added solemnly.

"I know that, Olivia," he said, as solemnly. "Doesn't it have a name?"

"I don't know."

She let him hold it when he asked, and watched him anxiously. Though he turned it close to his eye for as long as he could bear, he couldn't see a soundhole. No doubt it was obscured by the colours. "Why does it make that noise?" he asked.

She thrust the ball into her pocket, evicting an unwrapped toffee; then she stared at him, trapped. At once he was angry with himself. "I expect it's to go with the colours," he said. It wasn't any part of his job to spoil her toy.

Later, in class, he realized how oddly she had been behaving.

The children were painting mangers; he'd just told them the Christmas story. When the ball's song began abruptly, everyone started—everyone except Olivia, Tommy and Sharon, each of whom had one of the toys, and Linda, whom none of the others liked and who was pretending today not to be interested in anything of theirs. Cox searched for the owner of the toy; the sound had made Susan splash her painting, at which she was gazing tearfully. He saw Sharon opening her desk to hush the globe, which had apparently been singing to itself. "If it does that again you'll have to leave it at home," Cox said.

When he'd rescued Susan's painting he let her show him her brother's wedding photographs again. There was our Rose, wrapped in a pinkish-mauve mock satin bridesmaid's dress, like an expensive candy. Lovely, Cox agreed, ignoring the black roots of Rose's ash-blonde hair. Always be interested, he reminded himself. Kids always want to tell you everything.

But Olivia hadn't, he thought suddenly. She hadn't wanted to tell him anything.

He sat at his desk, frowning. The children always brought their new toys to show him. Only that afternoon Roy had handed him yet another model plane, which he had apparently constructed in the lunch-hour. At least, it had looked like that; Cox hadn't dared move his hands in case the wings came away. Olivia and Tommy and Sharon had competed for his attention in the past with new toys, yet none of them had shown him this latest toy, the singing globe. And kids always knew the names of their toys; why had Olivia avoided telling him?

He shrugged. No point in being disappointed. The less they depended on him the better, since he had them only for a year—so his colleagues always told him. Maybe his colleagues were right, maybe he was too involved with the kids. He began to pace again. "That's a beautiful painting, Susan," he said.

He was clearing up after class when he saw that Roy's desk was partly open. Propping the lid was the model plane. It wasn't like Roy to leave that behind.

120

He'd hurried away amid a small excited group, but even so he always carried his planes carefully home in a cardboard box, whatever else he might be doing. Cox hurried to the window in case he could call Roy back.

The boy was crossing the dark playground. The three children with him held globes in their hands; their faces bobbed about Roy, teeming luminously with colours. They'd passed through the gates before Cox could call out, and were hurrying in the opposite direction from Roy's home. Frowning, Cox tucked the plane into his own desk.

"Thank you," Roy said next day, and squashed the plane beneath his desk-lid, splintering a wing.

Ah well, Cox thought. Kids are fickle. At playtime Roy did nothing except gaze at his new toy. Could the globe harm the boy's eyes, or the other children's? Was it worth trying to break through the headmaster's blandness, to have their eyes examined? No, God forbid, Cox thought—few things were worth that effort. He'd ask the school nurse when she next visited.

By the end of the week every child in the class except Linda had a globe.

It was only a craze, Cox told himself. But it was worse than television. The children no longer played together. At playtime they stood or sat or leaned alone, gazing at the colours, though he noticed that they stayed close together, solitary yet grouped—his class, and a few of their friends. The other children avoided them, no doubt finding such inwardness uninteresting.

They must tell their friends where to buy the globes. But why had none of the other children bought them? Why hadn't he seen children from other schools with the toys? He'd never seen a craze so localized. Sud-

121

denly he was determined to know where the toys could be bought. He was sure they weren't helping the children's eyes.

Roy was standing at the edge of the group, intent on his handful of colour, the swooping petals of it thinning and transforming as they spiralled swiftly around the globe. "Where did you buy that, Roy?" Cox asked.

"Near us."

He was lying. He'd acquired the toy when Olivia and the others had led him toward their homes that night, away from his: Cox was sure. "Where exactly?" Cox said.

"Just a shop near us. I don't know what it's called."

Kids always know their neighbourhood shops by name. The rest of the group were pretending not to listen. For a moment Cox suspected theft. But the police would have notified the school of the theft of so many toys. Perhaps someone's relative owned the shop, perhaps the child wanted to choose who owned the limited stock of toys. Cox left them gazing at the flowering colours, beneath the dull snow-laden sky.

On Monday morning they made Christmas decorations. The sky gathered darkly, close to the window. Without warning Sharon said, "How do they get rockets into space?"

Now where had that question come from? Ah, Cox thought: the round decorations, the rounded shapes of the vehicles in *2001* on TV last night. He explained, and then they were all interrogating him as if their lives depended on the answers. When did the first rocket go? How far can they go? Why do they go? Olivia said, "How long will it be before they can reach the stars?"

An untypically sophisticated question, Cox thought—

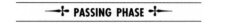

too much so for him. "Did you have a particular star in mind?" he countered.

She gazed at him, mouth ajar. Her forehead wrinkled, trying to squeeze out a speedy answer. But there was already an answer in her eyes. Susan said, "She doesn't know what she's talking about. She's just being stupid."

But Olivia was being nothing of the kind. Cox pondered as they made decorations silently, efficiently. It had been almost as if Susan had silenced the girl. For a moment, when Olivia had grasped his question, he'd been sure he had read *Yes* in her eyes. *2001* must have inspired her.

He was still pondering in the staffroom when Harry Turner said, "Have you calmed Susan Ellis down yet?"

Cox hadn't seen Susan excited since she'd shown him the photographs of Rose as a bridesmaid. "Why should I need to calm her down?" he asked.

"Don't tell me she hasn't told you. Her cousin told us all first thing. Our Susan's no longer the youngest of the litter. It's not like you to be late with that kind of news." He stared at Cox, thrusting his venous face close. "Don't look so hurt, man," he shouted. "You look like a bloody mother-in-law, expecting to be told everything."

It wasn't that. Cox's mind was held fast by the signs he'd ignored during the past few days. The children were changing. They were too quiet. Always, at this time of year, Cox felt as if the classroom were preparing for an enormous family Christmas party; but not this year. There was more to it than his feelings. A week ago Susan wouldn't have been happy until she'd told him about the new baby, nor would Roy have spoiled his plane. Something had happened to all of them, and Cox hadn't dared notice. Only habit had made him continue to see them as they had been.

He stared from the window, searching for them. They were standing about in a loose group. Linda was trying to join them, as she often did—pestering them, then losing her temper and starting a fight, running to complain that they'd hit her. She was the only one who hadn't changed, Cox thought: because she didn't have a globe. The globes were the culprits. It didn't matter how; they were. They must be banned. But it needed the whole staff to forbid them.

He couldn't talk about personality changes, for the others would think he was being subjective. He tried to persuade them to observe the toys more closely. He tried to convince them the globes harmed one's eyes. He tried. "Come on," he shouted at last, "I don't want my kids going blind."

"*Your* kids?" Harry Turner demanded. "Get married, Frank. You're turning into a bloody old maid."

"You mustn't mother them so much, Frank," Sheila Bliss said. "It'll be enough of a wrench for them to change schools at the end of the year."

"We aren't talking about the same thing."

"You know damn well we are," Harry Turner said.

Perhaps they were right, Cox thought after school. Perhaps he was so involved with the kids he was reading them too obsessively. Kids always tired of toys, after all. When they did, they'd be the kids he used to know again. If the toys were so dangerous they would hardly be sold.

Next morning it snowed. The children gazed out at the heavy slow flakes. "Haven't you ever seen snow

124

before?'' Cox said, but nobody even bothered to be cheeky. Still, they wouldn't have done much work anyway, not with the school Christmas party later. They all gazed out, except for Linda, who hadn't been clamouring for attention today. She held herself still, pressing her elbows against her waist, within the boundaries of her desk. She wouldn't tell him what was wrong. He hoped she would enjoy the party. Poor kid, nobody had ever let her adjust to the idea of her father in prison.

His class put up the trestle tables in the assembly hall, and were the first to sit down. Linda sat alone at the end nearest the tree, as if challenging people to sit by her. The other classes began to pour in. Cox helped direct them, dutifully ate presents of food or disposed of them unobtrusively, sang carols, stopped fights, danced with a succession of little girls. He wondered whether he should invite Linda to dance. He glanced toward her, but she was gazing at the tree. She was gazing at the tree in frozen horror.

When he saw her expression his stomach seemed to gape. ''What's the matter?'' he whispered to her through the uproar, trying to see. She was gazing at a tinsel decoration on the tree: just a tinsel ball. But as he stooped to talk to her, he saw it from her viewpoint: a swaying globe, full of hectic reflections of colour. At once he knew what had terrified her.

''All right, love,'' he said. ''Nobody can harm you here.'' He watched her as she sat frozen until the party was over, until her mother came to collect her for once. Then he went to see the headmaster.

To tell him what? Cox had seen what the globes were doing, but how could he convince the headmaster?

How could he tell him how Linda had been terrified, when he didn't know exactly himself? We must be certain, Mr. Cox. Feelings aren't enough. He told the headmaster he was sure that the toys were severely damaging the children's eyes.

"Remember we're trying to involve the parents, not antagonize them." For a moment Cox didn't know what the man was talking about. "We must beware of suggesting the toys they buy their children are dangerous unless we have definite proof. Without that we could find ourselves in a good deal of trouble. And we mustn't try to do too many other people's jobs. There are people employed to keep an eye on the safety of toys, you know."

He'd achieved his position by avoiding trouble; he always sidestepped it now. "I'm not sure the parents bought them," Cox said. "I don't think some of these families could afford it this close to Christmas."

"Have you proof of theft? No?" When he'd failed as a lawyer he had gone into teaching. "Bring me definite proof and I'll speak to the parents personally. You have my word. But vague feelings aren't much good to me, now are they?"

At the school gates Cox halted, the snow close and cold around his feet. Perhaps he should give up now. If it became known that he'd acted without the headmaster's authority, he would have made himself real trouble. But all he could see was the trapped terror in Linda's eyes. He began to trudge toward the street where Olivia, Tommy and Sharon lived.

The snow had stopped falling, but the drifts packed themselves around his boots. By the time he reached the tenement buildings, the wind against which he'd been leaning had glazed his cheeks. The wind rushed along the open corridor as Cox knocked again. The streetlamp's light swung wildly, raking the glittering wall.

"It's the teacher," Olivia's brother called, and slammed the door in his face. The wind pulled Cox's collar down. After a while Olivia's parents appeared, Tommy's behind them. "The children aren't here," Olivia's father said impatiently. "We're wrapping their presents."

"It was you I wanted to speak to." The wind tugged Cox's coat from his iced spine, but he ignored it. "I'm afraid we've discovered that these new toys they've got are dangerous," he said. "You know, the little globes. Very dangerous indeed. I'm going to warn the shop-keeper at once, if you'll tell me where I can find him."

"Do you know what he's on about?" Olivia's father asked his wife. "If she's been thieving I'll take the skin off her behind."

"I know what he means. Tommy had one," the boy's mother said. "It's not our fault if they play with things. We can't watch them all the time."

"Anyway, they have to learn for themselves," Tommy's father said.

Cox restrained himself. "Do you know where they bought them?" he asked the boy's mother.

"They didn't buy them anywhere. They found them up the road, on the waste ground." Cox hurried away down the corridor. "I think they took all there were," the woman called after him, "and they've thrown theirs away now."

So they had. Cox had nearly reached the waste ground, which began where the houses ended, when he saw three of the globes lying on the snow. They were only husks now, dark and empty. They'd run down, Cox thought gratefully. No doubt it had happened to all the globes by now. Nevertheless, he should make sure. He slipped stumbling off the pavement onto the waste, where patches of swung light scooped vainly at the treacherous dark snow. At once, thin amid the wind, cold and clear as the glaring stars, he heard the song.

Its source was buried in the snow, hundreds of yards out across the slippery hummocks, the disguised and unreliable bricks and rubbish, the traps of snow. But when Cox reached it, having almost crawled there on his frozen hands and knees, he didn't need the distant streetlamps. The swirling colours glowed clearly through their mantle of snow.

As he plucked the globe from the snow Cox realized that it had been resting against something else, in the shallow pit among the broken foundations.

He shook snow from the object. At once a second globe rolled from its mouth, singing. It was a metal cylinder about four inches long, almost weightless, rough and scarred; its closed end looked melted. As long as he held it globes dropped from its mouth, a dozen of them, two dozen. Their reflected colours scintillated wildly on the cylinder, demanding his attention, dismissing the miracle of the cylinder. The globes sang. They pleaded with him to look.

As soon as he did so the colours leapt inside his mind. The song ceased, having served its purpose. The colours adjusted his mind to their pace, starting thoughts and visions. They showed him the surrounding snow, the muted glow of each fragile crystal. They showed him the sparkling stars. Without looking away from the globe he felt one with the stars, with the immense cold distance to them, with the enormous dormant voyage to this spot. And this was the least of what his mind could hold. Just let the colours help him a little more. Just let him help the colours to live, let them have somewhere to live again, someone to live in, someone to build them a way for the rest of the colours to make the journey. Then the world would be full of colours, a wonderful sight. There was nothing to fear. There was nothing for Linda to fear.

His mind slipped that in, saving him. He recoiled, falling. He was back in the cold and the dark, as the colours tried to snatch his gaze again, chorusing beautifully. He picked up a brick and flattened them. When the flat discs continued to sing and to boil with colours he dug in the pit with the brick and stuffed the cylinder deep into the earth, hurling the crushed globes after it.

God knows what they were. Some kind of transmitter. The cylinder must have been the core of their vehicle, pared down by friction. They must have lost power en route from wherever they'd originated, otherwise the children could never have thrown the first ones away. They'd all be dead soon. Cox grinned viciously as he tamped earth down on them until their song was completely muffled.

His furious enjoyment was so hysterical he almost didn't hear the children.

They were converging on him from the street. There were dozens of them, shadows approaching unerringly over the dim snow. It must be his whole class and their friends. They were coming to find the rest of the transmitters. He must be sure they couldn't find them. He dodged behind a nearby wall.

He heard the children halt, and dig. They couldn't remember the location of the cylinder so accurately, it wasn't possible. They must be searching. He listened to the soft thump of thrown snow. The wind sifted the drifts around him. The children made no sound at all.

They'd ceased digging, and he was waiting for their squeaking footsteps to move away, when the colours began to encroach on his hiding-place, around both sides of the wall.

They must have seen him hide. Now they'd disinterred the globes and were using them to light their way to him. He wasn't Linda. If anyone had to be frightened it would be the children. He was still telling himself these things when the children appeared around the wall.

The globes were concealed in their hands. That was why their faces were glowing, exploding with colours. But they didn't respond to his commands, his appeals, his cries. The noose of light slipped over the snow around him, tightening; above it, above the darkness of their bodies, bobbed the translucently luminous faces—Olivia, Tommy, Sharon, all the rest, expressionless and writhing with colours. Now he knew why the globes they'd thrown away had been merely husks, for their hands were empty.

The chain of children was directing him between them now, along a narrow lane of closed glowing faces. He backed away from their silence, their stillness. It was only an X-ray effect, he thought, something like that. But where the bones of the skull would loom in an X-ray was only the turmoil of colours, streaming through the skin. He slithered backwards wildly over the snow, and tripped on the edge of the pit they'd dug for him.

The earth they'd piled ready followed him at once. His last sight was of the calm purposeful faces, glowing down hectically through a hail of earth and bricks. At once he saw that the movements of the colours were very much like the writing of larvae.

† A NEW LIFE †

Already he was blind again. But he was sure that someone had been peering at him. The glimpse was vague as the memory of a dream: the bright quivering outline of a head, which had had darkness for a face. Perhaps it had been a dream, which had wakened him.

Darkness lay on his eyes, thick as soil, heavy as sleep. It seemed eager to soothe his mind into drifting. He fought the shapeless flowing of his thoughts. He was near to panic, for he had no idea where he was.

He tried to calm himself. He must analyze his sensations, surely that would help him understand. But he found he could scarcely think. In the darkness, whose depth he had no means of gauging, his mind seemed to dissolve. He felt as though its edges were crumbling, as though nothingness were eating toward its core. He cried out wordlessly.

At least he had a body, then. He hadn't been able to feel it, and had dreaded that— The echo of his cry was hollow, but quickly muffled by walls quite close to him. The cry hadn't sounded at all like his voice.

If it wasn't his voice, then whose— He quashed that thought. His self-control was firmer now that some sense of his body had returned. He could feel his limbs, though faintly. They felt very weak; he couldn't move them. Clearly he hadn't yet recovered from his ordeal.

Yes, his ordeal. He was beginning to remember: being swept away and sucked down by the river, which had closed over his face with a hectic roar; the enormous weight of water that had thrust him down, into depths where his breath had burst out with a muffled agonized gurgling. After that, darkness—perhaps the darkness that surrounded him now. Had the river carried him here?

That was absurd. Someone must have rescued him and brought him here. But what place was it? Why would a rescuer leave him alone in total darkness, even when he cried out?

He controlled his gathering panic. He must be philosophical—after all, that was his vocation. Ah, he remembered that too; it comforted him. Perhaps, as he lay waiting for his strength, he could reflect on his beliefs. They would sustain him. But a twinge of fear convinced him that it might be wise to avoid such thoughts here. He subsided nervously, feeling as though the core of him were exposed and vulnerable. Chill sweat pricked his forehead in the close dark.

He must resign himself to his situation, until he knew more. He must be still, and await his strength. Sensation trickled slowly into his limbs. They seemed to form gradually about him: as though he were being reborn into a body. His mind flinched from that thought. For a moment, panic was very near.

He concentrated on sensation. His limbs felt enlarged, and cold as stone. As yet he couldn't tell whether these feelings were distorted by sickness. The threat of distortion troubled him; it meant he could be sure of nothing. It oppressed him, like the blinding darkness. He felt as though his brain and his nerves were drifting exposed in a void. Was he really blind?

How could near-drowning have blinded him? But while he scoffed at the idea, the darkness pressed close as a mask. What dark in the world could be so total? He remembered the face he had seemed to glimpse. That proved he could see—except that it was dim as a ghost of the mind, and perhaps had never been more than that.

The idea of being blind as well as enfeebled, in this unknown place, terrified him. With lips that seemed gigantically swollen, he cried out again, to bring the watcher back—if there had been one.

He heard his echoes blunder, dull and misshapen, against stone. Suddenly he was awash with panic. He struggled within his unresponsive body, as though he could snatch back the cry. He shouldn't have drawn attention to himself, he shouldn't have let the watcher know he was alive and helpless. All the fears which he had been trying to avoid insisted that his mind knew where he was.

For a while he could hear only the rapid unsteady

labouring of his heart. It seemed to become confused with its own echo, to imprison him with a clutter of muffled thudding. Then he realized that some of the uneven sounds were approaching. Very slowly, someone was shuffling irregularly toward him through the dark.

He squeezed his eyelids tight, and tried to keep absolutely still. He had lain so in his childhood, when the night had surrounded him with demons come to carry him to Hell. That memory appalled him. As he tried to ignore it, it clung to his mind. But he had no time to ponder it, for the footsteps had dragged to a halt close to him.

Something scraped harshly, and light splashed over him. The light was orange; it flickered, plucking at his eyelids. He felt as though the torch, whose sputtering he could hear, were thrust close to his eyes; he could almost feel its heat snatching eagerly at him. He shrank within himself, bathed in fear. He tried to hold his eyes still amid the flickering. At last the light withdrew a little, and metal scraped the dark into place again. The watcher shuffled away, dwindling.

Blinded once more, he lay in his cell. From the echoing stone, and the scrape of the spy-hole, he knew that was where he was. How could he have been imprisoned for trying to save a girl from drowning? Or had the authorities taken the chance to arrest him for his unchristian beliefs, which the University's theologians and his old parish priest had condemned? He tried to outshout his thoughts: no, his situation here had nothing to do with his beliefs, nothing at all.

His mind wasn't hushed so easily. It was as though fragments of thought that had remained from before his ordeal were settling together, clarifying themselves. Soon he would remember everything: far too much. Because he could almost remember it now, he realized that he didn't know his name. His panic seemed to sweep him deeper into darkness, where there was no sound, and no time. It felt like the beginning of eternity.

Perhaps it was. Before he could understand that thought, and give way entirely to terror, he made himself try to move. He must at least escape his helplessness. It might be possible to overpower the watcher. Surely it might be.

He strained. His limbs felt too large, and separate from him—as though bloated and stiffened by drowning. Of course that wasn't why they felt unfamiliar. The reason was— He struggled to reach his body with his mind, more to distract himself than in any real hope. His thoughts waited patiently for recognition.

At last, with a sigh that shuddered out of him as though he were relinquishing his life, he slumped helpless. At once his thoughts rushed forward. His body was beyond his control because he was dead.

The thought was terrible because it explained so much. It crushed him, as though the darkness had become stone. His blindness had robbed his mind of all defenses. If he tried to think, his philosophy led him straight to his fears. He was a child alone in the dark.

The image of the river was too vivid to be false. He'd been walking by the Danube when the girl had fallen in. He and another man had plunged in, to rescue her. The other man had reached her. But nobody had saved him; a hidden current had dragged him away and down, down, far too deep to have survived. The

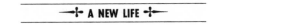

memory dragged him down now, into the relentless darkness.

As he walked, he'd been preparing the next day's lecture. Pythagoras, Plato, Kant. Could that have anything to do with his plight? No, he told himself. Of course not. Nothing. But he dreaded finding out where he was.

That was contemptible. He would know sooner or later, he couldn't change that; he must resign himself. If only he didn't feel so helpless! Perhaps, if he began very gradually, he could gain control of his body; if he could move just one limb—

He made himself aware of his limbs. They felt swollen, but not painful. A chill had gathered on them, from the surrounding stone. His back felt like a slab; his mind must be confusing it with the stone on which he lay.

He concentrated on his right arm. It felt distant, cut off from him by enormous darkness. He grew aware of the fingers. He tried to feel their separateness, but they were pressed together like a single lump of flesh, in a kind of mitten. They were bound, as was his entire body. Panicking, he strained to raise his hand. But it lay inert as meat on a butcher's slab.

Again he was a child in the dark, but more alone: even time had deserted him. He remembered lying in the darkness of his childhood, praying never to lose his beliefs, because if you died unbelieving you were doomed to eternal torment. His worst and vaguest terror had always been that the torment would be appropriate to the victim.

He fought against the current of his terror. How could he give up without trying all his limbs? His mind groped about, as though in a cluttered dark room; he was surrounded by jumbled dead flesh, his own. At last his awareness grasped his left arm.

It lay parcelled in its bindings, resting lifeless on the stone. That was how a mummy's arm must feel. Somewhere in there were nerves and muscles, buried in the meat: dead and unresponsive. He forced his mind to reach out. He was panting. His teeth scraped together, with a creak of bone that filled his skull.

He must reach out, just a little further. He could do it. Just one finger. But his mind was diffused by the darkness; it felt as though it were floating shapelessly in the meat. His thought of ancient history had stimulated it into babbling Pythagoras, Plato, Kant, von Herder, Goethe. All of them had believed— His mind writhed, trying to dislodge the thoughts. His violent frustration clenched his fist within its bindings.

For a moment he thought he'd imagined it. But his fingers were still moving, eager to be free of their mitten. He managed to subdue his gasp of triumph before it could reach the walls. He rested, then he raised his arm. It groped upward in the dark, brushing the chill wall beside him. Soon he would unwrap himself, and then— His arm rose a few inches, then shuddered and fell, jarring all its nerves.

He was still weak, he mustn't expect too much, must give it time. It took several tries to convince him that he couldn't raise his arm higher, nor move any other part of his body. His arm refused to bend, to reach his bindings; it refused to recognize him. His mind was a stagnant pool in a lump of unrecognizable flesh. He could no longer doubt that he knew where he was.

They had devised their torments well: allowing him

the illusion of triumph, the better to destroy all hope. Now came the torment of waiting helplessly, like a condemned man—except that the sufferings to which he was condemned would be eternal.

His childhood fears had told the truth. He should never have thought beyond them. For questioning his childhood faith, for believing that he would be reincarnated—the belief to which he had clung at the moment of his death, in the river—he had been condemned appropriately. To be reborn in an unfamiliar body, for unending torture: this was his hell.

They might keep him waiting for an eternity: that would be only a fraction of the time he had to suffer. They wanted his mind to fill with the tortures they were preparing, so that he could suffer them more fully. It did so. His helpless flesh could not even writhe. But he was sure they would make it feel.

His head throbbed with his pulse, as though all its flesh were pumping. Blood deafened his ears, like a close sea. Again it was a while before he could be sure that there were other sounds. The shuffling had returned, together with another set of footsteps, lighter and more purposeful. They were coming for him.

He sucked in his breath. He must stay absolutely still; they were waiting for him to betray himself. His teeth clenched, his lips trembled. Beyond the door, blurred sounds muttered. Though they resembled human voices, he was sure not all the distortions could be caused by the door. They must be discussing him. He tried to calm his face.

Metal slid, scraping. The torch peered in. Light danced on his eyelids, challenging him not to twitch. His breath swelled, harsh as stone in his lungs. At last a voice muttered, and the metal cut off the light. At once his breath roared out, appallingly loud.

Surely they couldn't have heard him, surely the sound of the spy-hole had muffled— But keys were scrabbling at the lock. His eyelids shook, his face worked uncontrollably; his treacherous mouth drooled. The door squealed open, and figures were standing silently close to him.

He must keep still. Eventually they would go away. He'd rest then, and try to free himself. But his face felt like a huge unfamiliar mask. It grimaced independent of his will. As it did so, one of the watchers hissed in triumph.

He had betrayed himself. There was no longer any reason to pretend, and his imaginings were worse than anything he might see. But when his eyes twitched open he groaned in terror. Beside the flames a stooped figure was peering down at him. One of its heads was covered with cloth.

The second figure must be a demon too, although it looked human: a thin young man with troubled eyes. His face stooped close, relentlessly staring. Then he stood up, shaking his head sadly.

That was surely not a demon's reaction. As the young man gestured the light closer, the man on the slab saw that the torch-bearer had only one head after all, and a hunched back. The light showed that the bindings of his limbs were bandages.

They had rescued him, after all! His fears and his paralysis were only symptoms of his sickness! He raised his arm, until it fell back feebly. The young man glanced at it, but continued to test the other limbs, shaking his head. The man on the slab tried to speak to him. But the sound that poured from his lips contained no syllables, no shape at all.

"Useless. Stupid. A failure," the young man muttered, almost to himself. "To think that I had that mind in my hands. How could I have reduced it to this?"

The shuffling man asked him what should be done. The young man told him indifferently, dismally, not even glancing at the victim he condemned. They went out, locking the darkness behind them.

Long after their footsteps had faded the man lay on the slab, straining to move his arm an extra inch, trying to pronounce three syllables, to prove his intelligence when someone returned. Just three syllables, the name he had heard the hunched man call his master: Frank-en-stein.

† THE NEXT SIDESHOW †

As Gray passed the locked kiosk, it began to rain. Water came pattering through the layers of autumn leaves still clinging to the trees; the dark lake plopped. Beyond the park, the auras of the tower blocks sparkled.

There was no use hurrying home. His key was locked in, and his wife wouldn't be home for at least half an hour; that was why he'd decided to stroll in the park. The kiosk rumbled like a drum. Its scrawny arch offered no refuge. Perhaps if the rain became too heavy he could shelter beneath the trees.

At least the hectic glistening made the paths more visible. The rest of the park was black and smudged as a soaked drawing. Clouds massed overhead, darkening

142

the night; they looked close and thick as foliage. Once he glimpsed the lights of the park road he would have his bearings.

Underfoot the path felt less like concrete than mud. Had the gardeners been moving earth, or had he missed his way? He stumbled onward, blinking; rain poured down his forehead into his eyes. Was that a shelter ahead, among the streaming trees? But there was no such building on his route home. Then he heard rain scuttling on metal. The dark shape was a caravan.

There were several, huddled like beasts beneath the trees. Raindrops traced veins through the dirt on their dim windows. Had the caravans any right to be there? They were robbing him of shelter. As he trudged past they rattled like maracas.

One pair of curtains was untidily parted. Beneath it, light slumped on the drowned twitching grass, and illuminated a section of a notice. Gray made out a few words: MAZE, FREAK SHOW, WELCOME. The letters squirmed under trickles of rain. Had the notice been laid there for passersby to read? It looked more as though it had fallen into the mud.

If the sideshows were open, perhaps he should take refuge there—but he'd never seen a freak show, and didn't intend to start now. He knew deformity existed; that was no reason to become involved in its exploitation.

As he picked his way along the squelching path, he started. Why? It had only been a glimpse of a face peering between curtains. He hadn't had time to distinguish it properly. It must have been his thoughts of freaks that had made the impression seem so unnatural.

The curtains had drooped shut now. Next to their caravan stood a low construction without wheels. Was it the freak show? No, he could just make out the sign that dangled slightly askew in the entrance: MIRROR MAZE.

The entrance was unlit. Within it, to the left, the cramped barred aperture of the paybox yawned, a cowl full of darkness. Sagging tendrils of his hair trained rain down his neck; his clothes and his eyebrows were sodden. He heard a new onslaught of rain rushing across the lake. Shivering, he dodged into the entrance.

Beside him a voice said, "Nowhere to go?"

He recoiled. He'd noticed a dim oval within the paybox, but had assumed it was painted on, or adhering to, the back wall. "I'm just sheltering," he admitted, faintly embarrassed.

The lower portion of the oval gaped. The voice was soft as the downpour, and almost as vague. "Why stand out here? Go in and take a look."

"It isn't really my kind of thing." No need to sound apologetic. "I don't think much of freak shows," he said more aggressively.

"Isn't that for you?" Gray couldn't decide if the tone was wistful or mocking. "Try the maze then, if you've half an hour to spare," the voice said softly as a hypnotist's. "That's something you won't forget."

Gray stared into the night. The park might as well have been miles underwater, for all that he could distinguish of it. "How much?" he said eventually.

"Any coin."

Was that meant as a gesture of goodwill? Gray found the choice embarrassing. Eventually he dredged up silver from amid the crowd of copper in his pocket. A hand reached beneath the grille. Why was it wearing a discoloured rubber glove so oversized that the rubber fingers splayed awry? But it wasn't wearing a glove. Gray couldn't help gasping.

The hand lay palm upward on the narrow counter—challenging his gasp, or demanding more money? Abruptly the fingers closed over the silver, like a plant trapping its prey. One finger pointed, as best it could, toward a door which was now outlined by a razor-edge of light. ''It's ready for you,'' the voice said.

As soon as Gray pushed open the door the oppressive heat seized him. His clothes felt humid and clinging; his coat began to steam. Sweat mixed prickling with the rain that coated his forehead. He stepped forward, and the door clicked shut behind him.

The first mirrors were dusty; his advancing reflection was vague. The ceiling loured perhaps a foot above him. Overhead a light jerked, buzzing; he could hear a swarm of them deeper in the maze. He was glad he hadn't paid more. Glancing back, he saw himself floating in a grubby mirror on the inside of the door, as though beneath mud.

He ventured along the narrow passage. If the building were as small as it had looked from outside, he would soon be through. Ranks of himself, stretching toward infinity on both sides, paced him.

He barred his way dimly. He could turn either right or left. Toss a coin? Responding to a memory of something he'd read—he couldn't recall where or in what context—about a left-hand path, he advanced that way. At once he had to turn several times, amid a crowd of his own antics. Shouldn't this trick him back where he'd started? But he must have miscounted his turns, for he emerged into a different narrow passage.

How was it different? A light hovered, buzzing inter-mittently. He squinted at the blurred mirrors. Sweat salted his eyes; he dabbed at them, and pulled off his coat. Why did his reflected movements look unnatu-ral? Suddenly he realized that all the mirrors were dis-torted.

Well, it was a gimmick. On one side of the passage he was inflated, a parody of pregnancy; on the other he was an hourglass with a face. Behind these reflections others gathered, far more bizarre. Had the proprietor tried to make up in oddity what the maze lacked in size?

Gray consulted his watch. He still had to find his way out. He strode forward. Swollen lumpy flesh uncoiled toward him, like a sluggish tenant of an aquarium. Which way at this mirror? Left again: at least he would know which direction not to take if he had to back-track.

His dusty face came nodding forward at him. It was almost as tall as he was, and squashed his body to ankle-height. This was fascinating. If the mirrors had been cleaner—if the huge bobbing face had been less blurred—he wouldn't have felt uneasy at all.

The only exit from this passage was to the left. He must be near the end now; there couldn't be much more of the maze packed into the building. Again he had to turn several times, always left. His skin felt hot, and grubby as the mirrors. The closeness of distorted flesh oppressed him.

Ah, here was a longer passage. Dim flesh squirmed at the far end; perhaps that mirror concealed the exit. He hurried toward it, glancing aside at the riot of distortions that filled the walls. When he peered ahead again, the glass at the end of the passage was blank.

The mirror must reflect only beyond a certain distance. Perhaps it was a final attempt to confuse victims of the maze. He strode at the mirror, ready to push it aside. Then he faltered. Dusty though it was, there was no doubt that it was a sheet of plain glass.

What had he seen beyond it, peering through? Nobody could look like that. Of course, there must be mirrors beyond; he'd seen a distant reflection of himself. Where was the exit? Irritably mopping his forehead, he turned left.

"You've never been in a maze like this."

He whirled. Flesh unfurled fatly around him. The voice was behind one or other of the mirrors; somehow the proprietor, or whoever had been in the paybox, had crept close to him. Gray kept his lips tight, though a pulse was leaping in his throat. He refused to admit he'd been startled.

"Not quite what you expected, is it? It's the same in all the sideshows. Never judge too hastily."

The tone of the soft voice seemed clearer now: oily, gloating. Was the proprietor trying to distract him, make him lose his bearings—because of what he'd said about freaks? All right, so the sight of deformity made him more uncomfortable than he'd admitted to himself: so what? He glared at his watch. He was damned if he'd ask the way out. He could bear ten more minutes.

He dodged through alcoves of mirrors: left, always left. Eyes peered at him from separated blobs of flesh; a tangle of disfigurements writhed around him. The buzzing of the unsteady lights seemed louder, as though a hive had burst. The relentless distortions made him dizzy. He had to halt and close his smarting eyes.

Surely he'd walked through the whole of the building by now. Was the proprietor sneaking mirrors into new positions, for revenge? Five minutes, then Gray would ask the way out—and by God, if the man didn't tell him he'd smash his way through.

As Gray opened his eyes, he saw movement at the end of the passage. Good God, what had it been? Himself, of course: he must have shifted inadvertently. Surely that was a parody of himself beneath the grime on the glass. Beyond the passage, to the left, he heard a click.

"These are the last of the mirrors," the voice said.

That must mean that he was nearly free. Gray headed for the voice, almost running. Overhead the buzzing jerked close; light twitched in the mirrors. He avoided glancing at the glass at the end of the passage. On the left a mirror had swung back. Shaking his head to clear it of dizziness, buzzing, oppression, he stepped through the gap.

The room within was smaller than a cell. An even dimmer light crawled feebly in a tube, stuttering. He peered at the rectangles of glass on the walls. Surely they weren't mirrors. Were they paintings?

"These are what I started with." The voice was

148

beyond the mirror at the far end—the exit, presumably. "A payment for services, that's what they were supposed to be. You meet strange folk on the road."

Gray faced one panel. No, it wasn't a painting; it was too luminous. Yet he could see the sun setting behind mountains. On one slope a small town bristled with turrets. How could the town glow more profoundly than the sky, as though with an inner light?

The image was receding. Momentarily he felt that he was watching it not through dusty glass but through a veil of mist. He stepped forward in pursuit, and the glass turned muddily opaque at once. Some kind of optical trick, nothing more—but he turned quickly to the other panels, into which images were retreating. Before he could reach any surface, all the glass was gray and dull.

"One more," said the voice.

One sheet of glass was not opaque: the one at the far end of the cell. He advanced, thrusting out his hand to shove it aside. His hand bulged in the mirror, pumped up like a balloon whose neck was his wrist. The glass made stumpy pillars of his legs, and dragged his head like soft wax halfway down his arm. His face— He couldn't take any more distortions; he felt giddy and nauseous. His eyelids fell shut.

When he heard the click, his eyes opened. The mirror had moved, exposing dimness. He stumbled quickly forward. He hadn't realized how dizzy he was; he could hardly walk or focus his eyes. But he must get out while he had the chance. Why? What was he escaping?

As soon as he was through, the mirror clicked shut. But it didn't feel like earth or concrete underfoot—

more like a patchy carpet. He blinked his eyes toward focus. Good God, he was in a caravan! He opened his mouth to protest; he struggled to regain control of his lips.

"That mirror made me what I am," the voice said.

Gray staggered about, trying to keep his balance, to raise his head. Suddenly he realized that it wasn't only dizziness that troubled him; the caravan was moving. It was crowded; he heard squirming in corners and on bunks. As his eyes slowly focused, he saw something like a hand holding a hand-mirror toward him. In its oval, the reflection of the caravan's interior was undistorted. By God, they'd better let him out; they wouldn't distract him with any more nonsense. But as he glimpsed the hand that he was thrusting out to ward off the mirror, he began to moan.

† LITTLE MAN †

Despite all his frustrations, Neal didn't go straight to the murder machine. First he played the pinballs, old friends he could make allowances for: Lady Luck and her costive straining to produce a ball, King Pin with his buzzing spastic flipper, Lucky Fruit who tricked you into thinking that your ball had reached the replay lane, until a kink in the wire rail let it slip out of play. He lost on all of them, and was glad he'd left the murder machine until last; it always calmed him.

It was December. A wind shrill as gulls swept up from the beach, along the stubby Bed & Breakfast terraces, and rattled the windows of The Mint. The fairground was closed for the winter; the rides huddled beneath canvas, enormous doughnuts, giant spiders;

the track of the roller coaster might have been the skeleton of a dinosaur which had crawled up from the beach to die. All summer Neal had ridden the dragon of the coaster, which had let him look down on people for once. They'd looked as small as the figures in the murder machine.

He pushed his coin into the rusty slot and gripped the sides of the machine. The miniature street—little more than a strip of plywood on which house-fronts were cartooned—was on a level with his face. As he leaned closer to the glass, the machine rocked forward on its lame front leg. Neither the movement nor his coin brought the performers out of hiding. Sometimes they arrived halfway through the show, like actors who'd sneaked out for a drink.

Here came a woman, juddering out of a hole in the left-hand end of the plywood, painted to resemble the mouth of an alley. She was daubed like a tin soldier— red cheeks, orange flesh, staring eyes; the buttons of her red coat were blurred dabs of white paint. A metal stalk protruded between her feet and jerked her along a track.

She was halfway down the street when a door popped open and the man with the knife pounced, dragging her inside. The door twitched shut. Beyond the polythene window a light glared red, and the squealing began, something like a siren, something like a mouse. Neal couldn't see what was happening beyond the crimsoned window, even when he pressed his face against the glass.

The light blinked out, the squealing ran down. That was all: no policeman today. No two performances

152

were the same, which was why the machine fascinated him—but when would it repeat the performance he was sure he'd once seen?

He stood back, rubbing the rusty stains from his hands. The sounds of the arcade came flooding back: the giggles of a little girl who was riding a mechanical turtle, the worn-out gunfire of an electronic rifle range, the unsteady tape of rock music, doggedly repeating itself. Again the world was bigger than he was—and it included school.

This year school was worse than ever. Half the masters seemed to delight in humiliating him, pretending they couldn't see him when he was standing up. "Where's that wild guess coming from? Oh, *there* you are." Some were cruel without meaning to be: the English master who'd persuaded him to appear in the end-of-term play, and even Neal's best friend Jim. "Come on, Conan," Jim said. "It's about time you came to the disco."

The disco was beside the promenade. Gulls swooped over the dark beach, their cries sharp as splintered ice, sharp as the creases of Neal's trousers. He wondered why he'd bothered to dress carefully, for the interior of the disco was chaotic with lights and darkness. When the girls approached he wondered why he'd bothered to come at all.

"Brought your little brother?" one shouted at Jim above the bombardment of music.

"Don't be funny, Di. This is my friend Neal. Karen, this is Neal."

"Hello down there," Karen said.

When the girls danced away Neal said, "I'm going."

Jim persuaded him to stay and found a partner whose friend let Neal buy her a Coke, then another, while he put off the moment when they would have to dance. Eventually they did, her lit chin hovering above him like a UFO, and he could tell that she'd taken pity on him. He left as soon as he could, hating himself.

If The Mint hadn't been closed for the night he would have gone straight to the machine. As he stalked home his surroundings looked like shrunken cartoons of themselves, hardly convincing: the locked fairground and Crazy Golf, the terraces that claimed to be full of hotels. Whenever he felt like this he seemed to be viewing the world through glass, a barrier that walled him into himself, and now that he'd reached puberty the barrier was more difficult to break.

It was no wonder. Apart from everything else, each rehearsal increased his dread of the end-of-term play. Why had he let himself be roped in? So that the English master would be on his side? He would pretend to be ill, except that his parents would know he was faking. They had enough to worry about now that two of the families who always stayed in the guest house were going abroad next summer. "You show them," his mother had cried when he'd told her about the play. All he was likely to show the audience, he thought bitterly as he slammed the ball into Lady Luck, was how much of a fool he was.

At least the murder machine distracted him. He couldn't time the performances, since he had no watch, but often the arcade seemed to recede, leaving him alone with the machine, for hours. Sometimes a policeman dragged the man in black into a doorway beneath a sketch of a police station's lamp. He was only pretending to drag him—his hand wasn't even touching the murderer's collar—and Neal imagined that as soon as they vanished beyond the door, the man in black dealt with him.

But what did the man in black do? Once, seconds after the scarlet woman had veered into his room, his door twitched ajar. Neal pressed his forehead against the glass. Murderer and victim were standing absolutely still—the man's eggshell face was turned toward Neal, the lifeless pinprick eyes and the mouth like a cut just starting to bleed—yet Neal had the impression that he'd stopped whatever he'd been doing. As the door snapped shut, he glimpsed red notches deep in the back of the woman's neck and in her left wrist.

That reminded him of something someone had once told him. Had it been his grandfather? What exactly had he said? He was no longer alive to be asked. Neal found himself trying to remember in class, the masters' voices receding, calling him back with questions he couldn't answer. "Use your little head," one master told him. Even the sarcasm couldn't reach him; the looming memory preoccupied him—until the end of term, until the play.

As soon as he emerged onto the stage, among the heaps of polystyrene and tinsel that were meant to look like snow, his heart sank. "There you are, Imp," said the pantomime magician, who was two years older than Neal. Neal's parents were sitting in the front row—his mother emitting small dismayed cries at any risqué jokes, his father frowning down at his fingernails—and so Neal had to scurry about squeaking and pretend he was enjoying it, while he was thinking: scuttle, scuttle, like a rat. He was sure the audience was laughing at him, not with him.

"You were the best," his mother cried afterward. His father nodded gruffly, not looking at him. Neal was glad to get away from them, but before he reached the dressing room he came face to face with Roger. Roger, who had a patchy mustache which failed to hide his pimples, often bullied Neal. "Hello, Imp," he sneered.

"Sod off."

Roger's pasty face reddened and began to quiver. "Don't you tell me to sod off," he said, grabbing Neal with hands like bunches of raw sausage. Neal kicked him viciously on the shin, leaving him howling. "I'll get you for that after Christmas, you little bastard."

Lashing out had relieved Neal's tension, but not enough. He was ready for the murder machine, too much on edge to dawdle over the pinballs. All along the main street, shops were for sale; the circus posters that patched their windows shivered in the wind from the beach. Even the survivors—gift shops full of plastic and cardboard, fish and chip shops called The Chef's, Maxim's, Café de Paris—were dark. The dusty window of the Midland Café was sown with dozens of dead flies.

Neal reached The Mint and halted, his fists and feet clenching. A little girl and her parents were at his machine.

Slamming open the glass doors of the Mint didn't scare them off. He flounced over to King Pin and stood muttering, too impatient to catch the balls with the flippers. No doubt the family thought he was cursing the pinball, not the girl. She seemed to embody all his frustrations; his resentment was scraping his nerves, resentment harsh as the miserly clicking of the fruit machines, the clicking that grew vicious in his ears, and louder. When she screamed, his first reaction was to smile.

She shrank away from the machine and held up her hands, which were smeared red. Behind her, Neal saw, the murderer's door was wide open. Before he could glimpse what was happening beyond, it snapped shut. If her parents hadn't been there he would have demanded to know what she'd seen, but they were ushering her out. "It's only paint," her mother said, which seemed further to upset the little girl. "Damned disgusting way to run a business," said the father, wondering perhaps where the paint had come from.

Though he hadn't had time to see into the murderer's room, Neal didn't resent the machine; it had got rid of the little girl, after all. The man's blank face with its pinhole eyes seemed friendly, the face of a beloved old toy. When the scarlet woman jerked into view, Neal observed that there were no red grooves in her neck or her wrist. He didn't understand, but he was prepared to wait for understanding.

Soon it was Christmas. His gifts came from The Money Spinner, one of the gift shops—a jigsaw, some pencils that changed color halfway through. His parents could afford only a dwarfish turkey, and his mother stiffened when he helped himself to a second mince pie. VACANCY said the sign in their front window, which was how the house felt for the rest of the holidays. Perhaps one day he would live somewhere that didn't make him feel so small.

He went for walks along the coast road. At low tide, sea and sand and clouds were bare elongated strips. Splinters of pale green sky were set into the clouds. The miles of flat narrow road were deserted except for gulls, some of which perched like vultures on the wastebins above the beach. He could almost see a figure in black in the distance, dodging along the road from bin to concrete bin, where litter writhed feebly in the wind. His grandfather had described something like that figure once, but why should Neal think he needed to visualize it clearly? For nights he was unable to sleep until he tired himself out with his efforts. Once, at the start of a dream, the figure jerked toward him, and he would have seen its face if the shrieks of gulls, disturbed by something on the coast road, hadn't wakened him. He was still trying to grasp it, no longer even wondering why he should, when the spring term began by confronting him with Roger.

Roger was gripping the rusty railings of the schoolyard as if they were spears. "Imp, imp, imp," he sputtered, like an engine trying to start. "I've been waiting for you, Imp. I've got something to give you tonight, behind the sheds."

"Leave him alone," Jim said. "Pick on someone your own size."

In some ways Neal was glad he'd intervened, for if it came to a fight between himself and Roger he knew he had no chance. But Roger sneered, "What are you afraid of, little boy? Afraid you won't be able to grow up?"

"Come on, Conan. Don't let him rile you."

"Just stop calling me that," Neal shouted. Suddenly he hated both of them. He stalked into the school, where Roger could do nothing.

All day Neal's mind and body felt as though they were seething. Every few minutes he had to wipe his hands down the sides of his desk. Yes, he would fight Roger; he'd kick him in the groin, as Jim had told him they did in the films. Suppose he missed? Roger would grab his leg and break it, he'd throw him down and kick his ribs in, stamp on his face—

"Wake up, Imp. Didn't you hear the question?" The master looked bored, unaware of any sarcasm; Neal was the Imp and that was all there was to it. At four o'clock, almost blind with self-disgust, Neal walked away from the school so quickly he might as well have been running.

The streets were cartoons, hardly even two-dimensional. Nothing was real except him and his thoughts. The sounds of The Mint fell away, leaving him alone with his friend. Murderer and victim disappeared into the room. Was there a shadow on the polythene window, a shadow that looked to be slicing and sawing? When the lights in the machine went out Neal lingered, imagining the tiny black-eyed face waiting in the dark, though it didn't seem so tiny once the dark grew as large as his feelings.

He had no idea how long he stood in front of the machine, nor what he was thinking. One thing was sure: that night he didn't think of Roger. He slept soundly, free of dreams. Next morning Jim told him that Roger had been knocked down on the coast road. He'd stepped in front of the car without looking, though he should have seen it coming hundreds of yards away; nobody could tell what had distracted him. Jim stared, then walked away, as Neal grinned.

Let him go: Neal didn't need him. Everyone had better watch out now, even Jim, if that was his attitude. The sarcasm of the masters no longer bothered Neal; the more they taunted him, he felt, the worse it would be for them, though he didn't examine why he thought so. His sense of security lasted until the night he went to see John Travolta in *Carrie*.

The Grand, which stood at the far end of the promenade, hadn't lived up to its name for years. Its ocher frontage looked built of sand, and ready to crumble. Ghosts of pre-war prices clung to the glass of the paybox. The manager stood at the top of the steps to the foyer; the knees and elbows of his dress suit were shiny as his toecaps. "About turn," he said to Neal. "This isn't for kids."

Neal's lips felt stiff and swollen, almost paralyzed. "I was eighteen last month."

"Aye, and I'm John Travolting. Scuttle away now, scuttle away." What made it worse was that he'd just let in two girls who Neal knew were barely fourteen, younger than himself. Worse yet, they were with Roger, who was hobbling boastfully on crutches. Crowing at Neal, the three vanished into the cinema.

Long before he reached The Mint he could see the shadow on the murderer's window, could hear the manager squealing in the tiny room. The shops on the main street were closed and dark, the bare road was the

160

colour of ice on a pond; worn patches of light lay
beneath the streetlamps. He was too deep in himself to
wonder at first why there were new dummies in a shop
that had been closed for months.

They weren't dummies, nor were they inside the
window. They were four youths, absolutely still and
silent except for the leathery creaking of their motorcycle gear. Were they waiting for him to turn his back
before they pounced? Sweat stung him like lit matches.

As soon as he'd walked past, his neck and his limbs
feeling stiff as china, they began to follow him. They
still made no sound except for the creaking of leather.
He didn't dare to run, for they could certainly outrun
him, but if a single shop had been unlocked he might
have dodged aside. Here at last was The Mint, but even
that was no refuge. One stopped the door from closing
with the metal toecap of his boot, and they crowded in
after Neal.

"At least something's open in this frigging town,"
one said loudly. They must have driven along the
coast, expecting the fairground to be open. They
quickly grew intolerant of the eccentricities of the pinballs; one kicked Lady Luck as though that would tame
her. Neal stood guarding the murder machine, which
he didn't want to play while they were there, in case
they came to watch.

The tallest of them sauntered over. "Go on, kid, put
your money in if you're going to." Neal could say
nothing, and the youth shoved him aside. "Let someone else have a go, then."

Neal tried to push him away from the machine.
Blood rushed to his head, which felt in danger of burst-

ing. His lips were huge and parched. "It's mine," he spluttered.

"Hey, look at this. He wants a fight." The youth picked Neal up easily, and holding him like a ventriloquist's dummy, talked for him in a shrill mechanical voice. "It's mine! It's mine!"

"That's enough." It was Mr. Old, who ran The Mint. "Put him down and get out, the four of you, or I'll call the police."

"Go on then," the leader said, dropping Neal so as to menace Mr. Old, "call the bloody police."

"That's exactly what I intend to do. You get away while you can, Neal. Run along now, go *on!*"

Neal could scarcely walk; his limbs were spastic with rage. He jerked along the street, looking for something to smash. Why couldn't it be the leader of the motorcyclists? When he saw the four emerging from The Mint, without a police car in sight, he fled. That night he lay sleepless for hours, punching the pillow in blind fury, clawing convulsively at the blankets.

In the morning he managed to control his rage, telling himself that tonight he would be alone with the machine. He'd play it until it showed him what he wanted to see, he vowed to himself, what had been troubling him since before Christmas.

Perhaps it was the vow that let him remember at last.

That afternoon one master was discussing local history: how the town had been built as a seaside resort for the Lancashire industrial towns, how it was dying of cheap Spanish holidays. Who could tell him more about the history of the town? Suddenly Neal could, and blurted it out as it came to him. "There was the man who started killing people when he came home from the first world war. He used to cut them up and leave the bits along the coast road. When the police caught him finally he tried to pretend he just had his hands in his pockets, only they weren't *his* hands.''

"No need to sound so pleased about it. I should try to put it out of your mind if I were you,'' the master said, and called on someone else, leaving Neal feeling guilty and furious because he did. He'd been pleased about remembering, he told himself, and then he wondered if it would make a difference to the machine. Perhaps he would be able to make out what happened in the reddened room, now that he knew what he was looking for.

No, it would not. That was clear as soon as he came in sight of The Mint and saw the pavement outside, littered with broken glass. Every machine was wrecked. The murder machine was a tangle of metal and plywood and jagged glass, amid which he could see no figures at all. He didn't need to ask who had done all this: he could hear their motorcycles roaring along the beach.

He trudged down to the promenade, with not the least idea of what he meant to do. Again he felt crippled by rage. Above the sea the moon hung, a plate whose pattern looked worn and blurred. At the distant edge of the sea, against the dim glittering of the waves, the motorcycles raced back and forth. "You bastards,'' Neal screamed.

The riders heard him. Now it was fear that crippled his legs. The cycles roared like animals which knew they had trapped their prey. The cycle with the tallest rider reared up and came for Neal. He watched helplessly as it raced toward him, leaving a track pale as a

163

snail's on the sand. The way the cycle grew as it sped closer seemed unreal as a dream, from which he wouldn't waken until it crashed into him. Even if he ran now, the rider would catch him long before he reached the houses. Nevertheless he tried to run, struggled to move his feet—just one and he'd be running. He was still fighting his paralysis when the rider leapt from the motorcycle.

For a moment Neal thought that he'd flung the cycle aside so as to grab him, then that the cycle had collided with a piece of driftwood lying on the beach, driftwood which had sprung up from the collision. But no, the dark shape wasn't wood, for it bounded over to the fallen rider, its movements stiff and jerky against the glittering of the waves. Confused, Neal thought it might be another of the cyclists—surely it must be a helmet, not the head, that looked pale as the moon—but only until it stooped to the groaning youth. Its movements were more assured now, the sawing of its right hand back and forth. Though the scene looked like a pantomime performed by dolls beside a toy motorcycle, the screams were appallingly human.

Neal ran from the coast road, afraid to look back. The streets were unreal, aloof from him, isolating him with his panic. The terraces of houses locked him out. Only the moon was menacingly vivid, a pale sketch of a face playing hide and seek with him among the houses.

By the time he reached home he was wheezing. He slammed the rusty gate behind him and stumbled along the few yards of path. He struggled to turn the key in the front door. Whatever had happened on the beach, it was nothing to do with him. He was home now, safe. The white face behind him was only the moon.

But there was a rusty movement, which might have been the gate—and a scraping voice, small but growing. "What shall we do next?" it said.

† NEEDING GHOSTS †

My wife Jenny was invaluable as always, though she didn't think this book as comic as I did. I'm grateful to John Mottershead of the Chapter One bookshop in Liverpool for the loan of his surname, and I've a special thank-you for Deborah Beale, my editor at Legend, without whose encouragement "Needing Ghosts" would never have been written.

For Penny and Alan
and Timmy and Robin
—some of my dark to find your ways through

He knows this dark. Though it feels piled against his eyes, it doesn't mean he's blind. He only has to lie there until he can tell where he is. As soon as his sense of his body returns he'll know which way he's lying.

He feels as though he has forgotten how to close his eyes and how to breathe. Perhaps he could shout and gain some idea of the extent of his surroundings from whatever happens to his voice, but he can't think of anything to say. The notion of shouting without words dismays him, and so does the possibility that he

166

mightn't know what he means to shout until he hears himself.

In any case, his sense of himself is beginning to gather. His arms are stretched out parallel to his body, his hands lie palms downwards by his sides. How thin they are! He's disinclined to raise them to his eyes in case he's unable to see them. The darkness must relent eventually, and meanwhile there's no call for him to move; didn't he take some trouble to achieve this peace? Now that he's aware of the remainder of his body—the outstretched legs, the upturned toes, the tight skin over the ribs—he ought to be able to enjoy lying still.

But the darkness is no longer absolute. It has begun to betray hints of shapes standing tall and immobile as if they're waiting to be seen. Those directly ahead of him appear to be draped in robes, and can't he hear voices whispering? He thinks of judges watching him with eyes that pierce the blackness, judges waiting for the dawn to reveal them and himself.

To his right he can just distinguish the profile of an open box at least as tall as himself. Hovering within it is an object which looks too oddly proportioned to be complete. To his left is an open horizontal box, from which shapes dangle as though exhausted by their struggle to emerge. He very much hopes that the whispers aren't coming from either box.

His clenched fists spread their fingers and reach out shakily on either side of him. By stretching his arms to their limit he can grasp the edges of the lumpy creaking mattress, and the action gives him some awareness of the room. Those aren't robed figures ahead of him, they're heavy curtains, and he's almost sure that if he parts them to admit more light he'll see that the figure hovering in the wardrobe, the stumps of its legs drawn up towards its handless monkey arms, is nothing of the kind.

He drags his hands over the mattress, the twang and contour and inclination of each buried spring reviving that much of his memory. He digs his knuckles into the frayed canvas and lifts himself into a sitting position, then he swings his legs into the dark and inches them downwards until his feet touch the floor. The carpet is so worn he can distinguish the outlines of the floorboards. Pushing himself away from the bed, he pads to the curtains, beyond which he can hear the whispering. He pokes his fingers through the gap in the musty velvet and heaves the curtains back.

The night is dancing just beyond the grimy window. Poplars whose foliage the dark has transmuted into coal toss their long heads in the wind. Several yards below him, wind ploughs through the grass of an unkempt garden hemmed in by trees. Inside the window, at the bottom left-hand corner of the lower sash, a draught plucks at a stray leaf caught in a spider's glimmering web.

So much for the whispering, however nearly articulate it sounds. He turns to the room. His suit is on a single hanger in the wardrobe, other clothes of his spill out of the chest of drawers. He isn't used to waking by himself in the dark, that's all. Now that he has risen he'll stay up and be on his way by dawn.

He trots out of the room and along the threadbare corridor without switching on the light above the stairs. When he tugs the cord in the bathroom, the light-bulb greets its own reflection in the mirror full of

white tiles, and something disappears into the plug-hole of the bruised bath. It must be a drip from the taps whose marble eyeballs bulge above their brass snout; he sees the movement glisten as it vanishes. He crosses the knotted floor and confronts himself in the mirror.

"There you are, old thinface. Nothing wrong with you that a blade can't put right." He's being deliberately cheerful, because he has never cared for the way electric light looks at this hour—too bright, as if its glare is straining to fend off the dark, and yet too feeble. His face resembles a paper mask, the skin almost smooth except for furrows underlining the sparse shock of gray hair, and almost white save for touches of pink in the twin hollows of the pinched cheeks, in the large nostrils of the long nose, on the pursed lips. The stubble on the pointed chin makes him feel grimy, and he ransacks the clutter by the sink for a razor.

Most of the stuff there seems to have nothing to do with him. At last he finds a razor folded into its handle among the sticky jars. He digs his thumbnail into the crescent-shaped nick in the blade, which springs out so readily that he can't help flinching. What's become of his electric razor? It's posing as another jar, its head clogged by talcum powder. On second thoughts, his chin can stay as it is. He stoops to the sink and wets his face with water from the right-hand tap, which grumbles like a sleeping animal, then he dries himself on a towel with a hole in it the size of his face. He lets down the dark with the cord and hurries to his room.

This time he switches on the light above the bed. The walls absorb much of the glow of the dim unshaded bulb, as their blurred surface seems already to have assimilated the pattern and the colours of the paper.

Though the room is spacious, it contains little furniture: the open wardrobe, the overflowing chest of drawers, the double bed with the bare mattress whose stripes trace the unevenness of the springs—just enough, he thinks, to show that it's a bedroom. He lifts his suit from the hanger and picks up the shoes which stand beneath it as though they've fallen from the legs. Once he is dressed he tours the house.

He shuts the lid of the massive toilet and rubs his hands with the ragged towel, and slams the bathroom door. Between it and his room are two bedrooms, an unmade single bed in each. Light through the lampshades steeps his hands in red as he fingers the wall-sockets to reassure himself that they're switched off. As he backs out of each room he turns the light off and shuts the door, holding on to the doorknob until he feels the lock click.

The clatter of his shoes on the uncarpeted staircase tells him how empty the large house is, and reminds him that he doesn't mean it to be empty for much longer. When he has opened the bookshop and customers are selling books to him as well as buying them, he'll store part of his stock in the disused bedrooms. He strides along the L-shaped hall to the kitchen, where fluorescent light smoulders in its tube while he screws the gas taps tight and grovels on the flagstones to examine the electric sockets on the perspiring brownish walls. He needn't check the room next to the kitchen, since it's locked. He looks into the rooms which, once their shared wall is removed, will house the shop. Chairs lean against a dining-table beneath the one live bulb of a chandelier, a lounge suite squats in front of a television tethered to a video recorder. He shuts the doors and lifts his rucksack from the post at the foot of the stairs. Hitching the rucksack over his shoulders, he lets himself out of the house.

The wind has dropped. The poplars are embedded in the tarry sky. Before he reaches the end of his over-grown path and steps into the avenue, his greenish shoes are black with dew. The road leads downhill between buildings which gleam white beyond the trees. Glancing back to reassure himself that he hasn't left a light on by mistake, he sees that all his windows are dark, all the curtains are open except those of the locked room.

He isn't surprised to find himself alone on the road; presumably nobody else rises at this hour. He can't recall ever having met his neighbours, but if they want to avoid him, that suits him. "He's out again," he announces at the top of his voice. "Lock your doors, hide behind the furniture, pull the blankets over your heads or he'll know you're there."

The only response, if it is a response, is the flight of a bird which starts up from among the trees and passes overhead, invisibly black, with a sound like the sweeps of a scythe. When it has gone and he falls silent, he thinks he can hear dew dripping in the trees beside the road. Spider threads caress his face, and he imagines the night as a web in the process of being assembled. He halts on the crown of the tarmac, wondering whether, if he's still enough, he may hear the whisper of the threads. Disturbed by the idea—not so much by the possibility of hearing as by his compulsion to try— he hurries down the avenue, wishing his tread were louder. He's glad when the landing-stage becomes visi-ble at the end of the road.

171

Perhaps he's too early. Though a ferry is moored there, it's unlit. As he continues downhill, the lights across the bay appear to sink into the black water. Just as he emerges between the last of the poplars, the lights vanish, and he feels as if everything—sky, trees, land, sea—has merged into a single lightless medium. The anchorage creaks as he picks his way to the gangplank and steps onto the deck.

All the stairways to the upper deck are roped off, and the doors of the saloons are locked. He's heading along the narrow strip of deck beside the front saloon when the gangplank is raised with a rattle of chains and the ferry gives a honk which vibrates through the boards underfoot. At once, as if the sound has started the waves up, water slops against the hull as the vessel swings out from the stage.

If it weren't for the occasional creak which reminds him of the sounds a house emits at night, he would hardly know he was on a boat. By the time the engine begins to thump, the ferry is well out from the shore. From the upper deck he would presumably be able to see the lights of his destination. He grips the sides of the prow and thrusts himself forwards like a figure-head, but can't determine whether the unsteady glow which appears to divide the blackness ahead is real or if it's only the flickering which often manifests itself within his eyelids when he can't sleep. He wedges his thighs in the V of the prow and watches the forest swallowing the buildings on the avenue. He finds the sight oddly satisfying, and so he doesn't face forward again until the ferry has almost gained the opposite side of the bay. When the steersman, a bust il-luminated like a waxwork by the instruments in the wheelhouse, closes down the engine, he slips out of his niche in the prow and turns to look.

The landing-stage is wider than the one below the poplars. Several figures are rising from benches in a shed at the back of the stage. Floodlights bleach the planks and show him the faces of those waiting—flesh white as candles, eyes like glass—as they crowd to meet him at the gangplank. He sidles past the crewman who has let the gangplank down, a burly man whose black beard so resembles the fabric of his Balaclava that his eyes and nose look false, and hurries across the shed to the exit ramp.

Only one of the several pay booths at the top of the tunnel is occupied. The woman inside it is poring over an obese dog-eared paperback, its cover hanging open to display a resale stamp. She waits until he pushes a pound coin under the glass of the booth before she raises her flat sleepy face, and he thinks of slot machines in the seaside arcades of his childhood, glass booths containing puppets which tottered alive if one fed them a coin. He's heading for the exit when she swivels on her stool and raps on the glass with the largest wedding ring he has ever seen. "Hey!"

If the fare has gone up, the least she can do is tell him by how much. But she only stares at him and thrusts her hand under the glass, and he thinks she's pointing at him until he notices the coin beneath her fingers. "Too rich to need your change?" she says.

"You've only taken for me."

"That's right, unless you're hiding someone in your bag."

"There's the bicycle."

She stares as if she's refusing to acknowledge a joke,

though she can see perfectly well what he means. He gestures at the barrier where he leaned the machine when she called him back, and then he realizes with a shock that he has left the bicycle at home. When he apologizes and reaches for the coin, her fingers recoil like caterpillars, and she bends the paperback open so fiercely that the bunch of pages she has read loses its grip on the spine and falls inside the booth. He knees the barrier aside and marches out of the tunnel, wondering what else he may have forgotten, feeling as though his very substance has been undermined.

On the far side of a broad deserted road, concrete office buildings catch fragments of the white glare of streetlamps in their multitude of windows. The interiors of the double-decker buses parked in a layby opposite the ferry terminal look moonlit. All six bus-stops have someone waiting at them.

As he crosses the whitened tarmac, the six men watch him silently. All of them are wearing dark suits—black, unless the light is altering the colour of their clothes as much as it's discolouring their faces. They don't respond when he nods to them, and so he does his best to ignore them while he looks for information. The timetables have been wrenched off the bus-stops; even the numbers on the metal flags have been rendered unidentifiable by graffiti which turns sevens into nines, nines into eights, whole numbers into mixed. Computer displays on the fronts of the vehicles announce destinations, but they bewilder him. Are the computers malfunctioning? Flicky Doaky, Eyes End, Cranium, Roly Polytechnic, View Hallow, Pearly Swine—he doesn't believe there are any such places; perhaps the names are jokes the drivers

crack after the buses stop running. The men by the
bus-stops seem to be waiting for him to react, and he
can't help suspecting that they're drivers. He leans
against a building to wait for someone to board a bus.

The men turn away from him and exchange glances,
and begin to call out to one another. "I'll be gone as
soon as I get my head down."

"I'll have mine under the covers before the sun's
up."

"Nothing like sleeping when the world's abroad."

"Nothing worse than not being able to switch yourself off."

"You mean the poor bat who couldn't even when he
was supposed to have retired."

"And wouldn't let anyone else."

It sounds like a prepared routine, passing systemati-
cally along the line from right to left, and he feels as if
they're talking at him. He's beginning to experience a
rage so black it suffocates his words when another man
emerges from a crevice beside him, an alley between
the buildings. This one must be a driver, though he is
almost a dwarf; he's wearing the uniform. He toddles
to the second bus from the left and turns a knob which
folds the door open, and it seems clear that he's the
person to ask. "Excuse me . . ."

The driver pokes a finger under the brim of his cap.
Thick spectacles make his eyes appear to occupy the
top half of his wizened face. "Not open yet. You don't
see anyone else moving."

True enough, all the dark-suited figures have turned
towards the conversation and are frozen in attitudes of
listening; some have lifted their hands to their ears. "I
only wanted to ask which bus goes to—"

He can't remember. With the loss of the word, his mind seems to shrink and darken. The driver is waiting as though only the word will release him, raising his eyebrows until his eyes fill the lenses of his spectacles. At last a name rises out of the dark. "To Mottershead. Which bus goes to Mottershead?"

"Never heard of it," the driver says triumphantly, and hops onto the bus. "Nothing called that round here."

"Of course there is."

The door flattens into its frame, and he's about to thump on the fingermarked glass when he realizes that Mottershead isn't the name of a place: it's his own name. He retreats and presses his spine against the facade of an office in which typewriters are hooded like ranks of cowled heads. He's restraining himself from turning his face to the concrete when the driver, having hoisted himself into the seat behind the wheel, reopens the doors and inclines his torso towards him. "Got another name for me?"

Mottershead thinks he sees a way out of the trap. "Where do you go?"

"Where it says."

Perhaps there really is a district called Eyes End. If Mottershead doesn't board the vehicle he'll be alone with five of the six men who witnessed his discomfiture, the sixth having flashed a rectangle of plastic at the driver and sat in the front downstairs seat. He watches Mottershead with interest and twirls a slow finger in one nostril. "That'll do me," Mottershead tells the driver, and steps onto the platform.

In his pocket is only a twenty-pound note and the change from the ferry. The driver reaches a long arm out of his metal enclosure and plucks the coin from Mottershead's hand. "You'll hear me call when you've run out," he warns, and starts the bus.

Mottershead is on the stairs when the vehicle backs at speed into the road and immediately lurches forward. He grabs the tubular banister and hauls himself to the top deck, where he lunges at the left-hand front seat and flings himself onto it, jamming his heels against the panel behind the destination indicator.

The view ahead has changed. Buildings which at first he takes for disused offices, their windows broken and their exteriors darkened by age, mirror one another across the road. They're warehouses illuminated by increasingly less frequent streetlamps. Black water glints beyond gaps to his right, while to his left, up slopes no wider than the bus, he glimpses unlit houses crammed together on both sides of alleys which appear to narrow as they climb. He'll make for any second-hand bookshop he sees which is open. Surely he won't be turned off the bus before it brings him to the shops.

When the bus slows, he presses his feet harder against the yielding metal. Two men are standing under an extensively annotated concrete shelter at the corner of an alley, and the foremost of them has extended a white stick like an antenna sensing the approach of the vehicle. The bus screeches to a halt, and Mottershead hears the door flutter open and the stick begin to tap upstairs.

He's assuming that the driver will tone down his driving, but the vehicle jerks forward like a greyhound out of a trap. He's preparing to help until he hears the man's companion following him upstairs. He watches their reflections on the glass in front of him as the man with the stick fumbles for the seat nearest the stairs and lowers himself onto it. Mottershead is shocked to see the companion mimic these actions, all the more so when he realizes why he is acting that way. Both men are blind.

If they don't leave the bus before Mottershead does they'll know that he didn't offer to help. The vehicle slows again, and he's afraid that the driver is about to summon him. No, someone is flagging the bus down, a man craning into the road from beside the stump of a bus-stop.

The door flaps shut, the bus lurches off between the warehouses. The new passenger takes some time to ascend the stairs. At the top he stands gripping the handrail, hunching his shoulders and turning his head tortoise-like. "Who's here?" he demands.

He's blind too. Mottershead is fighting a guilty compulsion to answer him when the man with the stick says, "It's us."

"Thought so. Nobody with all their senses is out this early."

He stumbles across the aisle and placing a hand on each man's scalp to support himself, sits down behind them. It doesn't matter to the three how dark it is, Mottershead reflects, and wonders what job they have been doing. What job has he retired from? Before he can start to remember, the thin voice of the newcomer distracts him. "Has he seen to the electricity?"

"Not him," says the man with the stick. "Too busy thinking of himself."

"Can't spare a thought for his people," his companion adds.

"You'd think he'd attend when they try to let him know his lights are going to fail."

"We'll have some fun when they're out."

"He'll be sorry he needs his eyes."

By now Mottershead's embarrassment has been supplanted by nervousness. Surely they wouldn't say such things if they knew they were being overheard. He peers along the passing alleys in the hope that he may see a better reason than his nerves to quit the bus. "I remember when the lights fused and I got my own back on my dad," the man with the stick laughs, just as Mottershead catches sight of a lit area beyond two consecutive alleys, which looks like the beginning of a wide street lined with shops. If he has to wait for any bookshops there to open, that's decidedly preferable to skulking in his seat. He plants his feet on the ridged floor and grasping the back of the seat, steers himself into the aisle.

The vehicle provides no means of communicating with the driver. Mottershead could shout or walk noisily, but he doesn't want to startle the three men. He tiptoes to the stairs and is stepping down carefully when the three turn their pale smooth faces to him. All their eyelids are closed, and so flat there might be no eyes behind them. As he falters on the stairs, the trio bursts out laughing.

They've been aware of him all the time. Enraged and bewildered, he clatters downstairs, shouting, "Hold on!"

The driver brakes as Mottershead gains the lower deck, and Mottershead has to grab the only handhold within reach—the shoulder of the man in the dark suit.

"What's the upheaval?" the driver complains. "Want to give us all a heart attack?"

"Sorry," Mottershead says to the passenger, apologizing not only for grabbing him but for discovering his secret. The man's upper arm is unyielding as plastic; he must have an artificial limb. As the bus regains speed Mottershead staggers to the door, seeing the lit area beyond another alley, shouting, "Let me off here."

"You're nowhere near where you've paid to go."

"This is where I want," Mottershead says through his teeth.

"I doubt it." Perhaps it's his stature, but the driver has begun to resemble a petulant child thwarted in a game. "You'll get no change," he says.

"Keep the change if it makes you happy. Just open up, or I will."

The driver slams the door open, and a wind howls through the bus. Mottershead is trying to prepare himself to accept the apparent challenge when the driver stamps on the brake, almost flinging him off the platform. "Thank you," Mottershead says heavily, holding onto the bus as he steps down.

The door flutters like a crippled wing, and he hears the driver announce to the passengers, "He thinks change makes us happy." The vehicle roars away, trailing oily fumes. When at last the fumes disperse it's still visible, a miniature toy far down the long straight road beneath the low black sky. Down there, perhaps because of the distance, the buildings look windowless. He watches until the bus vanishes as though the perspective has shrunk it to nothing, then he surveys where it has left him.

The nearest alley appears to lead into a lightless tunnel. He's about to retreat towards the openings beyond which he saw light, but then the streetlamp overhead allows him to guess at the contents of a window several hundred yards up the alley—piles of old books.

He steps between the walls and hears his rucksack scraping brick. As the darkness thickens underfoot, the sides of the warehouses tower over him. Where the alley bends beyond them, the window of the first building manages to collect a trace of the light, dimly exhibiting the books. He struggles along the passage, his rucksack flopping against the walls like a disabled pursuer, to the window.

He's tightening the shoulder-straps of the rucksack and skewing his head in an attempt to decipher the spines of the books when he becomes aware that the window belongs to a house. It could be displaying books for sale, but that seems increasingly unlikely as he begins to distinguish the room beyond the books. It's a bedroom, and although the disorder on the bed consists mostly of blankets, he can just discern a head protruding from them, its bald scalp glimmering. Before he has time to step back the eyes flicker open, and the occupant of the bed rises up like a mask on a pole draped with blankets, emitting a cry which seems to voice Mottershead's own panic.

Why has the tenant of the room stacked books in the window if he doesn't want to draw attention? Perhaps they're meant to conceal him, a rampart to keep out the world. It seems not to matter which way Mottershead runs so long as the figure he's disturbed can't see him.

By the time he regains some control of himself, he's out of sight of the main road.

Terraced houses crowd on both sides of him, their blackened curtains merging with the black glass of the windows. A hint of light between two houses entices him onwards. It's leaking from the mouth of an alley which should lead to the shops he glimpsed from the bus. The high uninterrupted walls of the alley bend left several hundred yards in, towards the source of the light. He dodges into the alley, glancing back for fear that whoever he disturbed may have followed him.

He's heartened by the sight which greets him at the bend. Ahead the alley intersects a lane of unlit terraced houses, on the far side of which it runs straight to a distant pavement illuminated by shops. He's crossing the junction when he notices that the right-hand stretch of the narrow lane is scattered with dozens of dilapidated books and sections of books.

This time there's no doubt that he has found a bookshop. The downstairs windows of two adjacent houses give him a view of a huge room full of shelves stuffed with books. There must be a light in the room, though it's too feeble to locate. Apparently the entrance is in the rear wall. He darts into the passage which divides the shop from the neighbouring houses, and the walls tug at his rucksack as if someone is trying to pull him back.

The passage leads him not to a street but to a back alley alongside the yards of the houses. He has to sidle between the walls to reach the alley he was previously following. There must be a dog in the yard shared by the houses which comprise the bookshop; he hears its claws scrabbling at concrete and scraping the far side of the insecure wall as it leaps repeatedly at him. He can only assume it has lost its voice. A protrusion on the gate of the yard catches a strap of his rucksack, and he almost tears the fabric in his haste to free himself.

At the alley he turns left, determined to find the entrance to the bookshop. As he reaches the junction he grunts with surprise. The glow from the shop has brightened, illuminating the lane, which has been cleared of books. The doorway between the windows is bricked up, but the glow outlines the glass panel of a door to their left. The panel bears an OPEN sign, and the door is ajar.

Since there's no sign of a proprietor or even of a desk where one might sit, Mottershead calls, "Hello" as he crosses the threshold. Only an echo of his voice responds, and is immediately suppressed by tons of stale paper, but the presence of so many books is enough of a response. They occupy all four walls to the height of the ceiling, and half a dozen double-sided bookcases extend almost the length of the shop, presenting their ends to him. There's barely room for him to sidle between the volumes which protrude into the dim aisles. Shrugging off his rucksack, he lets it fall beside the door.

He's becoming an expert, he thinks. One glance enables him to locate titles he has seen in every second-hand bookshop he has visited so far: *Closeup, The Riverside Villas Murder, The Birds Fall Down,* sets of the works of Dickens, dozens of issues of the *National Geographic,* editions of Poe. The material which appeals to him will be further from the entrance—books by countless forgotten authors whose work he can enjoy reviving for himself while he sits and waits for customers in his own shop. The notion that although these authors are either dead or as good as dead, he can choose to resurrect whatever they achieved as the fancy guides him, makes him feel as if he has found within himself a power he wasn't aware of possessing.

He's pacing along the line of bookcases in order to decide which aisle looks most promising when the spines of a set of volumes beyond them, on the highest of the shelves on the back wall, catch his eye. The fat spines, patterned like old bark and embossed with golden foliage, appear to be emitting the glow which lights the shop; presumably its source is concealed by the bookcases. Without having read the titles, he knows he wants the trinity of books. Since they're too hefty for even his rucksack to bear, he'll arrange to have them sent once he finds the proprietor.

He doesn't immediately notice that he's hesitating. What did he glimpse as he moved away from the door? He turns to squint at the shelves he initially dismissed, which contain the books whose titles he wouldn't have been able to discern in the gloom if they weren't already so familiar. He sees the book at once, and has the disconcerting impression that its neighbours have rearranged themselves, the better to direct his attention to it. He doesn't understand why the nondescript grubby spine should have any significance for him. Hooking one finger in the stall which the top of the spine has become, he drags the book off the shelf.

The illustration on the rubbed cover depicts a man's face composed of a host of unlikely objects. He hasn't time to examine it in detail, even though the face is familiar, because the words seem to leap at him. The title of the novel is *Cadenza,* and the author's name is Simon Mottershead.

He's able to believe it's only a coincidence until he opens the back cover. Though the photograph may be years or even decades younger than he is, the face which gazes up at him from the flap of the jacket is unquestionably the face he saw in the bathroom mirror.

He slams the cover as if he's crushing a spider. His mind feels dark and crowded; he knows at once that he has forgotten more than the book. He's tempted to replace it on the shelf and run out of the shop, but he mustn't give way to panic. "Is there anyone here but me?" he shouts.

This time not even the echo responds, though someone must previously have unlocked the door and picked up the books in the lane. Perhaps they're upstairs, but he wonders suddenly if the bookseller may be the person he disturbed by staring into the bedroom. On the whole he thinks he would rather not meet the proprietor face to face. He'll pay for the book in his hand and leave a note asking for the others to be reserved for him until a price has been agreed. He's relieved to see a credit card machine and a dusty sheaf of vouchers on a shelf to the left of the door. He gropes in his pocket for his credit card and a scrap of paper.

There's a solitary folded sheet. He shoves the book into the rucksack and unfolds the page. Two-thirds of it is covered with notes for a lecture. At the top, surrounded by a web of doodling, he has written the word LIBRARY and a date. "Today," he gasps.

He's supposed to be lecturing to a writer's group. His

mind feels as if it's bursting out of his skull. He digs his nails into his scalp, trying to hold onto his memory until he has recaptured all of it, but he can remember nothing else: neither the name nor the whereabouts of the library, not the name of whoever invited him nor of the group itself. Worst of all, he can't recall what time he has undertaken to be there. He's sure he will be late.

He grabs a pencil from beside the credit card machine. Flattening the page against the end of a bookcase, he prints the shortest message he can think of: PLEASE COMMUNICATE WITH ME RE THESE. He adds his details and then squirms along the nearest aisle, tearing off the message as he goes. Floorboards sag, books quiver around him and above him; he's afraid the bookcases will fall and bury him. By craning towards the tomes he's just able to insert the slip of paper into the niche formed by the florid cornice and the top of the leafy oaken binding. He leaves it dangling, a tongue blackened by his name, and retreats towards the door.

He still has to buy his own book. He pins a voucher with finger and thumb against the door, which shakes with every movement of the pencil as though someone crouching out of sight is attempting to fumble it open. A mixture of embarrassment at the small amount and determination to see his name clear makes him press so hard with the pencil that the voucher tears as he signs it, and the plumbago breaks. He lays the voucher in the metal bed and inserts his card in the recess provided, then he drags the handle over them to emboss the voucher. As the handle passes over his card there's a sound like teeth grinding, and he feels the card break.

He wrenches the slide back to its starting point and

gapes at the card, which has snapped diagonally in half. He opens his mouth to yell for the proprietor, having forgotten his nervousness, but then he sees that the lead which broke off the pencil was under the card when he used the embosser. Shoving his copy of the voucher into his pocket together with the pointed blades which are the halves of the card, he pokes his arms through the straps of the rucksack and flounces out, his book bumping his spine as if it's trying to climb the bony ladder and reinsert its tale into his brain.

The street is gray with a twilight which appears to seep out of the bricks and the pavement, much as mist seems to rise from the ground. A few windows are lit, but no curtains are open. He runs to the junction of the lane and the alley and listens for traffic. The only noises are the slam of an opened door and a rush of feet which sound as though they're stumbling over parts of themselves. Even if they're wearing slippers too large for them, their approach is enough to send Mottershead fleeing towards the light which was his original destination—fleeing so hastily that his impression of his destination doesn't change until he is almost there.

The area is floodlit, though several of the floodlights have been overturned on the flagstones with which the street is paved. Broken saplings strapped to poles loll in concrete tubs along the center of the street. All the shops are incomplete, but he can't tell whether they are being built or demolished. The figures which peer over the exposed girders and fragments of walls aren't workmen; they're plastic mannequins, more convincingly flesh-coloured than is usually the case. Vandals must have had some fun with them, because they are all beckoning to Mottershead, or are they gesturing him onwards? Their eyes are unpleasantly red. As he blinks at the nearest, he sees that someone has painstakingly added crimson veins to the painted eyeballs. A wind from the bay flaps the plastic sheets which have been substituted for roofs, the crippled saplings creak as their elongated shadows grope over the flagstones, and beneath the flapping he thinks he hears the creak of plastic limbs.

To his left the paved area curves out of sight towards the bay. To his right, perhaps half a mile distant, several cars are parked. Mustn't they be on or near a road? Willing the cars to be taxis, he sprints towards them.

The roofs stir as if the skeletons of buildings are trying to awaken. Whenever they do so, the arms of the mannequins wave stiffly at him. The state of the figures grows worse as he progresses: some are handless, and brandish rusty prongs protruding from their wrists; most are bald, and those which aren't wear their wigs askew—one wig as gray as matted dust has slipped down to cover a face. All the figures are naked, and sport unlikely combinations of genitalia, presumably thanks to vandalism. Some of the heads have been turned completely round on the necks, which are mottled as senile flesh. As he passes one such figure it falls forward, rattling the bars of the stranded lift which cages it, and Mottershead claps a hand to his chest as he runs onwards.

By now he can see that each of the three cars is occupied, but suppose a car dealer has propped mannequins in each of the drivers' seats? The roofs writhe, and a bald figure sprawls towards him, leaving behind the hand with which it was supporting itself on the back of a solitary dining-chair. Its head is hollow, and empty now that the contents have scuttled away behind a girder. He would cry out if he had breath to do so, but surely there's no need, since the three figures in the cars have sat up and turned towards him. He's no longer alone with the tread, floppy but not quite barefoot, which is following him. He lunges for the foremost vehicle, his eyes so blurred with exertion that he can hardly see the door. He's near to panic before his fingertips snag the handle. He levers it up and collapsing into the back seat, slams the door.

However much of a relief it is just to sit there with his eyes closed, he has to keep moving. "The library," he wheezes.

Either the driver is taciturn by nature or he's losing his voice. "Which?"

At least he seems unlikely to trouble Mottershead with the unnecessary chatter typical of his species, but his response sounds suspiciously like an imitation of Mottershead's wheezing. "The one where a writers' group meets," Mottershead says, interrupting himself twice as he tries to catch his breath.

He's hoping that his words will provoke a further question which may help him clarify his thoughts. To his surprise, the driver starts the car, and Mottershead lets himself sink into the seat, feeling sponge swell to meet his hands through the torn upholstery. When he's no longer aware of having to make himself breathe, he looks where he's going.

The incomplete buildings have been left behind. The car is passing a concrete edifice guarded by railings like fossilized branches and twigs. Despite the stained glass in its windows and the inscriptions carved in scrolls over its broad doorway, it must be a factory rather than a church. Coaches whose windows are impenetrably black are parked inside the gates, and thousands of people, all of them carrying objects which may be tool-kits or briefcases and wearing brightly coloured over-alls in which they resemble overgrown toddlers, are marching silently into the building. He's trying to de-cipher the writing on the carved scrolls when he no-tices that the driver is watching him.

As soon as Mottershead's gaze meets his, the man fixes his attention on the road. Mottershead is almost certain that he is wearing a wig, a curly red wig twice as wide as his neck, above which it perches like a parasite which has drained all colour from the rings of pudgy flesh. The mirror seems to have lent the reflec-tion of his eyes some of its glassiness, for although they're bloodshot, they look dollish—indeed, a flaw in the mirror makes the left eye appear to have been turned inside out. Mottershead throws himself about on the seat in order to shed the rucksack and reach his book.

He intends it both to help him ignore the driver and to revive his ideas for the lecture, but as soon as he reads the opening sentence—''He knows this dark''—he feels threatened by remembering too much. He skims the long paragraphs packed with detail as the unnamed protagonist listens to the dawn chorus and lets his other senses feast on his surroundings, which sunlight and his awareness of his own mortality are beginning to renew. Mottershead has glanced at only the first few pages when the memory of labouring on the novel begins to form like a charred coal in his mind. He leafs back towards the dedication, but slams the book shut as he realizes that the taxi is drawing up at the curb.

He stuffs the book into the rucksack and stares about him. He's outside the entrance to a shopping mall, a pair of glass doors framed by several neon tubes whose glare is almost blinding. "I want the library," he protests.

"You've got it."

There's no doubt now that the driver is mimicking him, raising the pitch of his voice as Mottershead did. "I can't see it," Mottershead says furiously.

"You will."

Mottershead imagines his own voice being forced to rise as the argument continues, topping the driver's mimicry until it becomes a screech. He flings himself out of the vehicle, almost tripping over the rucksack, and thumps the door shut with his buttocks. "What are you expecting?"

"Two and a big pointed one."

Mottershead produces the twenty-pound note. He wishes he could see the driver's face, but the neon at the entrance to the mall has dazzled him. "I've nothing else to offer you."

"You delight me," says the driver in exactly the same tone. He takes the note and hands Mottershead a smaller one. Mottershead keeps his hand extended, though he isn't looking forward to a repetition of the driver's touch; the man's stubby fingertips seem to lack nails. He's still awaiting change when he hears the driver release the handbrake, and the taxi speeds away.

"Wait," Mottershead neighs, struggling to see past the blur which coats his eyes. He slaps his empty hand over his face and stands crying, "Stop thief." The noise of the vehicle fades more swiftly than the blur, until he begins to plead for his sight. Nothing matters more than being able to see. He'll let the driver go if he can only have his vision back.

At last his sight clears. He's beside a dual carriageway, across which the long blank slab of the shopping mall faces acres of waste ground where a few starved shrubs are decorated with litter. Above the carriageway, red lamps grow pale as the light of a glassy sun glares across the waste. There's no sign of the taxi among the traffic which races along both sides of the road, turning grey with the dust in the air. "Good riddance," Mottershead mumbles, and glances at the note in his hand. It's his own twenty-pound note, except that part of it—about an eighth—has been torn off.

He emits a shriek of rage and swivels wildly. His movement prompts the doors of the mall to slide open, and he veers towards them, through an arch of massive concrete blocks reminiscent of the entrance to an ancient tomb. As soon as he has passed between the doors they whisper shut behind him.

The mall is three floors high. Shops and boarded-up rooms surround a wide tiled area on which more than a dozen concrete drums containing flowers and shrubs are arranged in a pattern he can't quite identify. The air is full of a thin sound, either piped music or the twittering of the birds which are flying back and forth under the glassed-in girders of the roof. Escalators rise from the center of the open space, bearing figures so stiffly posed that they look unreal. He barely notices all this as he dashes into the nearest shop.

It's a video library called Sammy's Hat. Cracked plastic spines are crammed into shelves on the walls which flank the counter, behind which a large man is watching a dwarfish television. IF YOU'RE NOT HAPPY WITH OUR SERVICE is printed on the front of his T-shirt, which is close to strangling his thick arms and neck beneath his raddled sprawling face. Cassette boxes flaunt their covers behind him: *Don't Look in the Oven, The Puncturer, Rude and Naked, Out of His Head.* . . . He acknowledges Mottershead only by ducking closer to the television, which is receiving the credits of a film called *Nasty, Brutish and Short*. "Is it possible for me to phone?" Mottershead says over the buzzing of kazoos.

The shopman's small eyes narrow. "Anything's possible here."

"I mean, may I use your phone?"

The man heaves a sigh which sets boxes rattling on the shelves. "What's it all about?"

"I've been robbed," Mottershead declares, waving the remains of the note. "I just paid my taxi fare with this, and this is what the cabby gave me back."

On the tiny screen a stooge who appears to be wearing a monkish wig is poking two fingers in another's eyes. The shopman throws himself back in his high chair, chortling so grossly that his saliva sizzles on the screen. "Come and see this," he shouts.

A woman tented from neck to feet in gingham squeezes through the doorway behind him. Her ruddy face is even wider than his, her eyes smaller. Mottershead assumes that the shopman has called her to watch the film until the man points at the torn note. "That's what he got when he tried to pay his fare with it," he splutters.

Mottershead feels another screech of rage building up inside him, but it will only waste time; he won't be penniless for long—he'll be paid for the lecture. "Forget it," he says when the hoots and howls of the couple squashed behind the counter begin to relent. "Just tell me where the library is."

The woman lifts her dress, revealing thighs like a pink elephant's, to wipe her eyes. "You're in it, you poor bat."

"Not this kind. The kind with books."

Mottershead intends his tone to be neutral, but the shopman flings himself like a side of beef across the counter and makes a grab for his lapels. "You watch what you're saying to my daughter. Nothing in here to be ashamed of. Stories, that's all they are."

Mottershead backs out of reach, his ankles scraping together. "You don't deserve to have eyes if that's the best you can do with them," he says from the door.

He's hoping to seek help from a security guard, but none is to be seen. At least the couple aren't following him; they've begun to pummel each other, whether because they are choking with laughter or for some more obscure purpose he can't tell. He dodges into the next shop, a tobacconist's full of smoke. "Can you tell me where the library is?"

"At the end."

Perhaps the tobacconist is distracted, having apparently just singed his eyebrows while tuning the flame of a lighter. When Mottershead runs to the far end of the mall he finds only a baker's. "Library?" he wheezes.

"Who says?" The baker looks ready to turn worse than unhelpful. He's digging his fingers into a skull-sized lump of dough which has already been shaped; a swarm of raisins oozes from the sockets into which he has thrust his thumbs. "Thanks anyway," Mottershead blurts, and retreats.

One of the assistants in the adjacent toy shop leaves off playing long enough to direct him. "Up and through," he says, and points a dripping water pistol at him.

Mottershead is afraid that the gun may fire and ruin his lecture notes, and so he makes for the escalators as the assistants recommence chasing one another through the chaos of toys, which reminds him more of a playroom than of a shop. The extravagant threats they're issuing in falsetto voices fade as the deserted stairs lift him towards the roof.

Like the vegetation in the concrete tubs, on closer examination the birds beneath the roof prove to be artificial. Several birds are pursuing their repetitive flights upside down, presumably because of some fault in the mechanism, and their maker appears not to have thought it necessary to provide any of them with eyes. Mottershead finds the spectacle so disagreeably fascinating that he's almost at the top before he notices that someone has stepped forward to meet him.

She's a woman in her sixties whose hair is dyed precisely the same shade of pale blue as her coat. Her flat chest sports a tray which contains a collecting-tin and a mound of copies of the badge pinned to her lapel. "Is there a library here, do you know?" he pleads.

The woman stares at him. Perhaps she didn't hear him for the mechanical twittering of the birds. The escalator raises him until he's a head taller than she is, and he repeats the question. This time she lifts the tin from its nest of badges, which say PENSIONERS IN PERIL in letters red as blood, and rattles it at him. "I'm sorry, I've no money," he complains.

Of course, her stare has grown accusing because he's still holding the remains of the twenty-pound note. "This won't be any use to you. Can't you tell me where the library is?"

Her only response is a look of contempt, and he loses his temper. "Take it if you've got a use for it," he shouts, "if it'll persuade you to answer a simple question."

As he begins to shout, a security guard emerges from a greetings-card shop and jogs towards them. "Is he bothering you?" the guard demands.

"I just want the library," Mottershead wails, seeing himself as the guard must see him, towering over the pensioner and yelling at her. Worse, she has taken the torn note from him, and now she has found her voice. "He tried to pass me this."

"Because you insisted," Mottershead protests, but the guard examines the note before he turns on Mottershead, frowning through the shadow of his peaked cap. "I'd say you owe this lady more than an apology."

"I tried to tell her I've no money." Receiving only stares from both of them, Mottershead blunders on: "I'm a writer. I'm needed at the library. They've asked me to talk."

"So have we," the guard says ponderously. Then the woman stuffs the note into her tin and waves Mottershead away as if he's an insect she can't be bothered to swat, and the guard grasps his shoulder. "Let's make sure you end up where you're wanted."

Before Mottershead quite knows what's happening,

he is being marched to the end of the mall above the baker's. Here, invisible from below, is an unmarked door. When the guard leans on a bellpush beside it Mottershead starts to panic, especially when the door is opened by another man in uniform. He can't judge how large the cell beyond the door may be; it's piled with cartons, and the passage between them is scarcely two men wide. The guard who is holding him tells the other, "He claims you've invited him to talk."

"Show him through, love. He'll be for the sound-proof room."

He flattens himself against the cartons to make way, and the guard pats his plump buttocks with one hand as he shoves Mottershead into the passage. The uni-formed man purrs like a big cat and rubs himself against the cartons. "Hold on," Mottershead protests, "where are you taking—" Then the guard reaches past him and opens a door, and Mottershead's voice booms out beyond it, earning him so many disapproving stares that he would retreat into the cell if it weren't for the guard.

He's reached his destination by a back door. The library is as large as the mall, and disconcertingly simi-lar, except that the walls which overlook the escalators are occupied by books rather than by shops. In front of the multitude of books are more tables for readers than he's able to count, and all the readers are glaring at him. "Where am I meant to go?" he mutters.

"I'll walk you," the guard says, and steers him left-wards. "What was the name?"

"Simon Mottershead." He raises his voice in the hope that some of the readers will recognize his name, but they only look hostile. He lets himself be ushered past the tables, trying to think how to convince the readers that he isn't a miscreant. He hasn't succeeded in dredging up a single thought when the guard marshals him left again, through a doorway between shelves of Bibles and other religious tomes, into a room.

The room is white and windowless. Several ranks of seats composed of plastic slabs and metal tubing face away from the door, towards a single chair behind a table bearing a carafe and a glass. About twenty people are scattered among the seats, mostly near the table. Before Mottershead can make for it, the guard leans on his shoulder and sits him in the seat nearest the door. "Simon Mottershead," the guard announces.

Every head glances back and then away. "Not here," someone says.

The guard's hand shifts ominously on Mottershead's shoulder. "I'm Simon Mottershead," Mottershead stammers. "Isn't this the writers' group?"

This time only a few heads respond, and someone murmurs, "Who?" Eventually a woman rumbles, "Are we expected to turn our seats to you?"

"Not if I'm allowed to move." Mottershead heaves himself to his feet and shrugging off the guard's grasp, turns to stare him away. The man's expression is so disappointed and wistful that it throws him, and he blunders towards the table, struggling to unstrap his rucksack.

He hears the guard trudge out and close the door, though not before admitting someone else. The latecomer is wearing either slippers or sandals. The sound of footsteps flopping after him makes Mottershead feel pursued, and unwilling to look back. By the time he's past the table, the newcomer is already seated. Mottershead drags the chair out from the table and dumps his rucksack on the floor, seats himself, lifts the inverted glass from the carafe and turns it over. When nobody comes forward to introduce him, he looks up.

He can't identify the latecomer. He doesn't think it would be any of the several elderly women who sit clutching handbags or manuscripts, more than one of which is protected by a knitted cover. It might be one of the young women who are staring hard at him and poising pencils over notepads, or it could be one of the men—not those who resemble army officers, red-faced with suppressing thoughts, but possibly the lanky man who reminds Mottershead of a horse propped on its tailbone, his shoulders almost level with his ears as he grips his knees and crouches low in his seat, or the man whose bald head gleams behind a clump of hatted women. Every eye is on Mottershead, aggravating his awareness that he's meant to speak. He tips the carafe and discovers that it contains not water but a film of dust. "As I say, I'm Simon Mottershead," he says, fumbling for his notes.

His audience looks apathetic, perhaps because they're wondering why he is digging in his pockets with both hands. He must have dropped his notes in the bookshop; his pockets are empty except for the voucher and the pieces of his credit card. "What would you like me to talk about?" he says desperately.

The faces before him turn blank as if their power has been switched off. "Tell us about yourself," says a voice he's unable to locate or to sex.

He feels trapped by the question, bereft of words. "Are you married with children?" the voice says.

199

"Not any more."

"Did it help your writing?"

At least Mottershead has answers, even if they're almost too quick for him. "Nobody except a writer knows how it feels to be a writer."

"Harrumph har*rumph* humph," a red-faced man on the front row responds.

"I'll tell you how it felt to me," Mottershead says more sharply. "Every day I'd be wakened by a story aching to be told. Writing's a compulsion. By the time you're any good at it you no longer have the choice of giving it up. It won't leave you alone even when you're with people, even when you're desperate to sleep."

By now the faces are so expressionless that he can imagine them fading like masks moulded out of dough. "When it comes to life," he says, anxious to raise his own spirits as much as those of his audience, "it's like seeing everything with new eyes. It's like dreaming while you're awake. It's as if your mind's a spider which is trying to catch reality and spin it into patterns."

"Harrumph harrumph harrumph," the red-faced man enunciates slowly, and leaves it at that. As Mottershead ransacks his mind for memories which don't cause it to flinch, the voice which raised the question of his family speaks. "What's it like to be published?"

"Not as different from not being as you'd think. I used to say I expected the priest at my funeral to ask, 'Did he write under his own name?' and, 'Should I have heard of him?' and, 'How many novels did he write a year?'"

He's hoping to provoke at least a titter, but no face stirs. "Weren't you on television?" says the voice,

which is coming from the bald head beyond the hats.

"Exactly," Mottershead laughs. Then the questioner sidles into view, and Mottershead sees that he wasn't suggesting another cliché but trying to remind him. "If you say so," Mottershead says unevenly. "I told a story once about someone who thought he was."

He's closer than ever to panic, and the sight of his questioner doesn't help. He assumes it's a man, even though the appearance of baldness proves to have been achieved by a flesh-coloured hairnet or skullcap. Although nearly all the flesh of his long mottled face has settled into his jowls, this person isn't as thin as he seemed to be when only his scalp was visible; it's as if he somehow rendered himself as presentable as possible before letting Mottershead see him. His large dark eyes glisten like bubbles about to pop, and his unwavering gaze makes Mottershead feel in danger of being compelled to speak before he knows what he will say. "Everything's material, anything can start a story growing in your head. Maybe that's our compensation for having to use up so much of ourselves in writing that nobody wants to know us."

The man with the unconvincing scalp looks suspicious and secretly gleeful. When his piebald mouth opens, Mottershead stiffens, though the question sounds innocent enough. "Do you still write?"

"I'm leaving it to people like yourselves."

If that signifies anything beyond allowing Mottershead to feel relatively in control, it ought to encourage the audience, but the questioner smiles as if Mottershead has betrayed himself. The smile causes the upper set of the teeth he's wearing to drop, revealing gums black as a dog's, and he sticks out his tongue to lever the teeth into place. "Wouldn't they give you a chance?"

"Who?"

"The powers that decide what people can read."

Everyone nods in agreement. "I don't think we need to look for conspiracies," Mottershead says, feeling as if his own teeth are exposed.

"Then why did you stop?"

He means stop writing, Mottershead assures himself. The man's gaze is a spotlight penetrating the secret places of his brain. "Because it wasn't worth it. It wasn't worth my expending so much of myself on creating the absolute best I was capable of when nobody cared that I had."

"Don't you think you were lucky to be published at all?"

The man's whitish tongue is ranging about his lips; he's begun to look as mentally unstable as Mottershead suspects he is. Genius may be next to madness, Mottershead thinks, but so is mediocrity and worse where creativity is concerned. "I think that's up to my readers to judge, don't you? What does anyone who's read my books think?"

He lets his attention drift heavenwards, or at least towards the twiglike cracks and peeling leaves of plaster which compose the ceiling. When his pretense of indifference produces no response, he sneaks a glance at his audience. How can the back of every head be facing him? "Anyone who's read anything," he says, attempting a careless laugh. "Someone must have read me or I wouldn't be here."

The pink-scalped man rears up, knotting the belt of

his faded and discoloured overcoat which could almost be a dressing-gown. "Remind us," he says.

At least the audience is watching Mottershead, but without warmth. "I expect you'll have heard of *Cadenza*. That was my best book."

"Who says?" his interrogator demands.

"I do." There must have been reviews, and surely Mottershead had friends who gave him their opinions, but where those memories should be is only darkness. "I put everything I could into that book, everything of myself that was worth having. It's about the last days of a man who knows he's dying, and how that gives new life to everything we take for granted."

"How does it end?"

"I'll tell you," Mottershead says, only to discover that the dark has swallowed that information too. "Or perhaps," he corrects himself hastily, "someone who's read it should."

The doughy faces slump. Nobody has read the book. The bald man's stare is probing his thoughts, and he feels as if he's being asked, "Why do you write?"— being compelled to answer, "Life is shit and that's why I use up so much paper." He's opening his mouth— anything to break the breathless silence—when it occurs to him that he needn't try to recall the end of the book. He grabs the rucksack and placing it on the table in front of him, unfastens the buckles and opens it towards his audience like a stage magician, displaying the book. "This is me."

It's immediately obvious that he has blundered somehow. "I beg your pardon. This is I," he says, and when their expressions grow more unconvinced: "This am I? I am this?"

The bald man smirks. "I should let it drop."

They needn't quiz Mottershead's grammar; some of them are bound to have perpetrated worse. Losing patience, he lifts the book out of the rucksack, and sees why they are unimpressed. His name is no longer on the cover.

He must have torn the jacket as he shoved the book into the rucksack; it's missing from the front of the book and from the spine, the binding of which is blank. He pulls the rucksack open wide, then forces it inside out, but nothing falls from it except a scattering of soil.

"Har-rumph," the red-faced man pronounces, and several heads nod vigorously. The man with the pink scalp, whose cap fits so snugly that it seems to be flattening flesh as well as any hair which the headgear conceals, stares wide-eyed at Mottershead. By God, he'll show them he wrote the novel. He throws it open, its cover striking the table with a sound like a lid being cast off a box, and finds that the copyright and title pages have been torn out. There's no trace of his name in the book.

He can still display the photograph inside the back cover, which seems impatient to be opened; he's almost sure that he feels the book stir. He picks it up gingerly, but the table beneath it is bare. He squeezes the volume between his hands and lets it fall open.

Perhaps his face is on the flap, but so is an object which has been squashed between the cover and the flyleaf. It's where he remembers the photograph to have been, and the markings on its back are very like a face. Despite its having been flattened, it retains some life. He has barely glimpsed it when it raises itself and staggering rapidly off the book, drops into his lap.

He screams and leaps to his feet, hurling the book away from him. The object, whose welter of legs makes it appear to have doubled in size, falls to the floor and scuttles through a crack beneath the skirting-board. The audience watch as if they're wondering what further antics Mottershead may perform in a vain attempt to shock them into responding. "I'll show you," he babbles. "Just talk among yourselves while I fetch a book."

Everyone turns to watch him as he heads for the door, forcing himself to walk as though he doesn't feel like running out of the room. Nobody speaks while he struggles with the mechanism of the door, twisting a knob above the handle back and forth until he hears a click and the door swings open. He steps out and pulls it to behind him.

Either the readers at the tables are engrossed in their work or they're consciously ignoring him. He tries to move quietly as he hurries from shelf to shelf. Once he identifies the fiction, surely he'll find one or more of his books. All the shelves on this side of the top floor, however, hold only books about psychology and religion, arranged according to some system he can't crack. He sidles between two tables, ensuring that he doesn't brush against the Bible readers in front of him, and his buttocks bump a woman's head. She's wearing a rain hat which resembles a shower cap, and it must be this which deflates at the contact, but it feels as if her skull has yielded like a dying balloon, a sensation so disconcerting that the apology he means to offer comes out as, "My pleasure." Feeling at the mercy of his own words, he blunders to the edge of the balcony and clutches the handrail.

If the fiction is shelved separately from the rest of the stock, he can't see where; every visible shelf holds books larger than any novel, some as thick and knobbly as full-grown branches. As he runs on tiptoe to the down escalator, a sprint which takes him halfway around the perimeter, a few readers glower at him. They would be better employed, he thinks, in complaining about the muffled shouts and thumping, presumably of workmen, which have begun somewhere offstage. A stair crawls out of hiding and catches his heel with a clang that reverberates through the library, and he sails down to the counter.

This is shaped like a symbol of hope, a curve stretching out its arms towards a way of escape. Two librarians with wide flat faces sit shoulder to shoulder at a table behind it, poring over a tome Mottershead takes to be an encyclopedia of wild animals. He shuffles his feet, clears his throat, knocks on the counter. "Hello?" he pleads.

One librarian removes her steel-framed spectacles and passes them to her colleague, who uses them to peer more closely at an illustration. "Better see what the row is," he suggests.

Mottershead is framing a tart response when he realizes that even now they aren't acknowledging him. Both raise their heads towards the shouts and pounding on the top floor. They could be identical twins, and their stubbly scalps, together with the pinstripe suits and shirts and ties they're wearing, seem designed to

confuse him. "Can you tell me where to find your fiction?" he says urgently.

"You'll see none of that here," the man says without a glance at him.

"What, nowhere in the library?"

"Only books about it," says the woman, watching someone moving behind and above him.

"No need for fiction here." The man returns her spectacles to her and nods at the book on the desk. It isn't about animals, Mottershead sees now; it's a study of deformed babies, open at a picture of one which appears to have been turned inside out at birth. He's glad to be distracted by a commotion on the top floor, a door releasing a stampede of footsteps and a protesting hubbub—glad, that is, until he looks up.

The uniformed man who admitted him has let the writers out of the room, which is indeed almost sound-proof. They glare about the balcony, ignoring the shushing and tutting of the readers, and then several women brandishing handbags and manuscripts catch sight of Mottershead. They rush to the edge and point at him, crying, "He locked us in."

"I didn't mean to," Mottershead calls, but the entire library responds with a sound like the dousing of a great fire. "I didn't mean to," he confides to the librarians, who shrug in unison as the writers march away along the balcony. "Where are they going?"

"Where they came from, I expect," the male librarian says with satisfaction.

"But I haven't finished!" Mottershead flaps his arms, and is preparing to shout when the stares of all the readers gag him. Perhaps he should let the writers go, especially since he hasn't found a book to show them—but then he realizes what he has forgotten. "I haven't been paid."

The female librarian tosses her head to prevent her spectacles from slipping off her rudimentary nose. "No use telling us."

"Don't you know who's in charge?" Mottershead begs.

"You want his holiness."

"The reverend," her colleague explains.

He's pointing at the red-faced man whose entire vocabulary seemed to consist of false coughs, and who is making his way around the balcony towards the down escalator. Mottershead pads to the foot of the escalator, trying to phrase a demand which will be polite but firm. "I believe I'm to be paid now," he rehearses as the red-faced man comes abreast of the escalator. The man marches past without sparing it or Mottershead a glance.

Is there another public exit besides the one beyond the counter? Mottershead groans aloud and sprints to the opposite escalator, dodging irate readers who twist in their seats and try to detain him. He grabs the banister, which squirms as it slithers upwards, and runs up the lumbering stairs.

As soon as he's three stairs short of the balcony he manages to heave himself onto it, using the banisters like parallel bars. The only door he can locate leads to the stockroom through which the guard brought him, but he shouldn't be searching for a door. The red-faced man is returning to the down escalator, having replaced a hymn-book on the shelf.

Mottershead clutches his aching skull. It will take him several minutes to run around the balcony to that escalator, by which time his quarry may well have left the building. "Reverend," he calls desperately. "Reverend! *Reverend!*"

The man seems not to hear him. Either he's experiencing a vision which renders him unaware of his surroundings as he rides towards the ground floor, or his title is only the librarians' nickname for him. Mottershead lurches onto the stairs which are climbing doggedly towards him and clatters down, shouting "Hey! Hey! Hey!" Even now the red-faced man doesn't look at him, though all the readers do; many of them start to boo and jeer. While Mottershead is managing to outrun the escalator, his quarry is descending at more than twice his speed. He's only halfway down when the red-faced man steps onto the floor and strides past the counter.

"My fee," Mottershead screams. He lifts his feet and slides down, his heels clanking on the edges of the steps. At the bottom he launches himself between the tables, where at least one reader sticks out a foot for him to jump over. The exit barrier is executing a last few swings, but the red-faced man is already past the doors beyond it. Mottershead is almost at the counter when the man with the pink scalp steps into his path.

"Let me pass," Mottershead cries, but the man widens his glistening eyes and stretches out his arms on either side of him. The librarians are miming indifference, gazing at the roof. "Get away or I'll buffet and belabour you," Mottershead snarls, which earns him admonitory looks from the librarians. He's poising himself to rush his tormentor when the man steps forward, soles flapping. "Reverend Neverend said to give you this."

Is he protracting a joke which the librarians played on Mottershead? But he's waving an envelope, brown as the wrapper of a book which has something to hide. Mottershead suspects that it contains a text he has no desire to read. "Didn't he even have the grace to serve me with it himself?" Mottershead says for the readers to hear, and snatches the envelope. At once he realizes that it's full of coins and notes.

The writers must have held a collection for him. Feeling exposed and clownish, he slips the envelope into his pocket, which he pats to convince himself that he hasn't dropped the envelope, and wills the readers to forget about him. As he tries to sneak past the counter the messenger detains him, seizing his elbow with jittery fingers whose nails are caked with ink. "Can I talk to you?"

"You have done."

"That was for the others. I want to talk about ourselves. We've lots in common, I can tell."

"Some other time," Mottershead says insincerely, trying to pull away without looking at him.

"There won't be."

"So be it, then." Mottershead attempts to stare him into letting go, but can't meet the other's eyes for long; they look as if being compelled to see too much has swollen them almost too large for their sockets. "I want to be left alone," he mutters.

"You know that's not possible."

Mottershead feels black helplessness closing around his mind. He wants to lash out, to thump the man's scalp, which he's sure is plastic disguised not quite successfully as flesh. What would it sound like? The temptation dismays him. "Will you have a word with this person?" he says at the top of his voice.

The librarians frown at him. "What about?" the female says.

"About your dress code, I should think."

The man with the replaced scalp is wearing slippers on his bony feet, and if his buttonless garment belted with old rope isn't a dressing-gown, it might as well be; certainly he's wearing nothing under it except striped trousers like a sleeper's or a convict's. The librarians are still frowning at Mottershead, but he doesn't care, because his outburst has caused his tormentor to flinch and loosen his spidery grip. He pulls himself free and knees the barrier aside, shouting, "I think you've got some explaining to do" to freeze the man in case he considers following. He closes both hands around the heavy brass knob of the door and having opened it just wide enough to sidle through, drags it shut behind him.

He has emerged onto an avenue lined with shops beneath a heavily overcast sky. Display windows shine between treetrunks as far as the eye can see. Though the upper storeys are obscured by foliage, it seems to him that the shops have taken over a variety of buildings; through the leaves he glimpses creatures so immobile they must be gargoyles, bricked-up towers like trees pruned to the trunk, domes green as mounds of moss. To his right, in the distance where the trees appear to meet, the sky is clear. He heads for the light, hoping it will help him think.

Before long he sees that he's approaching a bookshop, its windows full of paperbacks as bright and various as packets in a supermarket. Wasn't *Cadenza* put into paperback? The thought of the book makes him shriek through his teeth; he has left the damaged copy and his rucksack in the library. He can't imagine going back, but perhaps there is no need. Dodging the bicycles which are the only traffic, he crosses to the bookshop.

The glass doors are plastered with posters for a book called *Princess the Frog*. The sight of eyes bulging at him from beneath crowned bridal veils confuses him, so that he grapples with the doors for some time before discovering that the right-hand door is locked into position. He shoulders its twin open and thinks he has cracked the glass. No, he has dislodged a poster, which the door crumples and tears. He steps over it and moves quickly into the shop, pretending he was nowhere near.

Fiction is ranged around the walls. Anything by Mottershead ought to be on the shelves at the back of the shop. He's passing the authors beginning with I when someone catches up with him. "May I help you?"

"I'm looking—" Mottershead begins, and then his voice goes to pieces. He has been accosted by a frog in a wedding dress. In a moment he's able to distinguish that the frog is an elderly woman, her leathery skin painted green with the makeup she has used to make her mouth seem wider. She's holding the poster he crumpled. "I can find it myself, thank you," he says in a voice so controlled it feels like stifling a belch.

"Keep in mind that we're here."

Whether that is meant as a warning or as an offer of

assistance, it aggravates the hysteria he's trying to sup-
press. She has drawn his attention to her colleagues
who are scattered about the shop, all of whom, including at least one man, are dressed as bridal frogs. This
must be part of a promotion for the book which is
advertised on the posters—there's a mound of copies
of the book draped with waterweed beside the cash-
desk. He clutches his mouth as he begins to splutter,
and flees deeper into the shop.

The letter M covers the whole of the back wall. He
has the impression that the patterns formed by the
print on the spines spell out several giant versions of
the letter. His name is almost at floor level—Mottershead, in several different typefaces. He digs his fingers
into the tops of the pages and tugs at the four books. No
wonder nobody has bought them if they're wedged so
tightly on the shelf. He manages to tip them towards
himself until he's able to grasp the corners of the
spines. He heaves at them, and without warning they
fly off the shelf and sprawl across the floor.

Before he can pick them up, the frog bride who origi-
nally followed him hurries over. "It's all right," Mottershead tells her, feeling his mirth coming to the boil
again as he stoops to gather the books. "I'll buy these
if you'll give me a carrier bag. I wrote them."

Does she think he's lying? Disapproval stretches her
mouth wide enough to render her makeup redundant.
"Look," he says, no longer wanting to laugh, "I assure
you—" Then he sees the covers of the books he's
claiming to have written, and his jaw drops.

The author's name is undoubtedly Mottershead; it's
spread across the covers in large raised capital letters.
The first name, however, is printed small to fit between

the thighs of the girls whose naked bottoms are embossed on the covers. The books are called *Eighteen, Seventeen, Sixteen* and *Fifteen,* and it's clear from the faces gazing over their shoulders that these are the ages of the girls. He doesn't need to focus on the author's first name to be certain that he could never have entertained such thoughts, let alone admitting them on paper—but how can he convince the princess frog?

"You'd better have them before I do any more damage," he mumbles. If she will only take them, he'll run out of the shop; he no longer cares what she thinks of him. But she shakes her head violently and clenches her greenish fists, further crumpling the poster, and two of her fellow frogs close in behind Mottershead. "Trouble?" the male bride croaks.

"The author of those items claims to have found them on the shelf. One wonders who must have put them there."

"I was mistaken. I didn't write any of these books."

The frog with the poster stares incredulously at Mottershead. "Seems not to know when to stop telling tales," remarks the fattest of the frogs.

"Do I look as if I could be responsible for this stuff?" Mottershead cries. "Why would I be trying to buy books I'd written myself?"

The frogs snigger. "Some people will stop at nothing to promote themselves," says the one with the poster.

Mottershead is overwhelmed by rage which feels distressingly like panic. He tosses the books into the air and is on his way to the exit before they come down. He's fleeing past the shop when the three booksellers appear at the window, hopping up and down and croaking inarticulately as they wave the books at him.

214

All the passing cyclists begin to ring their bells as if to draw attention to him, and he dodges behind a chestnut tree, turning up his collar to hide the parts of his face he can't squash against the trunk.

As soon as the bellringing slackens he dodges out from behind the tree and hastens along the avenue, trying to outrun a sound which he has begun to suspect is concealed by the jangle of bells. He has passed only a few buildings, however, when he comes to a bookshop which has taken over a cinema. The compulsion to find himself on the shelves is stronger than ever. Glancing along the deserted pavement, he darts into the shop.

Several life-size cut-out figures, presumably of authors rather than of film stars, loiter inside the entrance. Shelves like exposed girders branch across the walls of the gutted auditorium, and the floor is crowded with tables piled with books: *The Wit of the Answering Machine, 1001 Great Advertising Slogans, Inflate Your Brain*. . . . Beside the propped-up figures two young blondes deep in conversation lean against the cash-desk. "She has the same hair as me," one says in a voice light as tissue, and her friend responds: "I'll have to try it sometime." There's something rather forbidding about the perfection of their young faces, their long eyelashes and blue eyes and pink lips, their unblemished flesh; he can't help thinking of the oldest of the models on the covers of the books he has just disowned. The thought sends words blundering out of his mouth. "Can I have one of you?"

They turn to him with expressions so identically polite that their spuriousness disconcerts him. "I mean, can one of you show me where you keep Simon

215

Mottershead? Not the Mottershead who has fantasies about girls of your age and younger," he adds hastily. "The one who wrote *Cadenza*."

None of this has made any visible impression on them. He feels as if their perfect surfaces are barriers he can't touch, let alone penetrate. "I'm talking about books, you understand," he says. "I want you to show me some books."

The assistant to his left glances at her colleague. "Better call the manager."

"Is that necessary?" Mottershead says. Apparently it is; before he has finished speaking, the other girl presses a button on the desk. A bell shrills somewhere behind a wall, and a woman several years older than those at the desk but made up to look the same age rises like a figure in a pop-up book from behind a table. "What can I do for you?" she asks Mottershead.

"I'm waiting for the manager."

"I am she."

"Then you can help me," Mottershead says, trying to sound friendly and apologetic and amused by his gaffe. "I'm after Simon Mottershead."

"We have nobody of that name here."

"Books by him, I mean."

"We have none."

"Can you show me where to look? I believe you, obviously," Mottershead lies, "but you've such a large stock . . ."

The woman grunts as though he means that as an insult. "You'd be wasting your time. I know every book in this shop."

Why is she trying to get rid of him? He feels as if the blackness which threatens his mind is darkening the shop, gathering like smoke under the roof. His surroundings, the faces of the women included, appear to be losing depth. "At least," he says desperately, "you must have heard of Simon Mottershead."

"I won't pretend I have."

The blackness is about to swallow everything around him except her cut-out face and those of her assistants. "Well, now you've met him," he almost screams, and flounders towards the exit, which he can barely locate. As he makes a grab for the door, someone who has been waiting in the doorway steps into the shop. It's the man with the false scalp.

He blocks Mottershead's path and holds up one hand, and Mottershead loses control. Seizing the man's shoulders, which feel loose and swollen, he hurls him aside. The man falls headlong, taking two of the propped-up figures with him, and Mottershead is sure he's exaggerating his fall, playing to the audience, who emit cries of outrage and run to help him up. Mottershead knocks over the rest of the propped-up figures to hinder any pursuit and kicks the door shut behind him.

He's hardly out when he sees another bookshop through the trees. Its sign—EVERYTHING WORTH READING—is so challenging that he can't resist it. Fewer bicycles are about, and they and their bells seem slowed down. He sprints between them and peers around a treetrunk. When he sees nobody following him he scurries to the third bookshop.

The frontage seems altogether too narrow for the shop to accommodate the stock of which the sign boasts. On the other hand, if the proprietor's standards are higher than those apparent in the other shops, shouldn't this one stock Mottershead's work? He pushes open the black door beside the dim window occupied by a few jacketless leathery books. A bell above the door sounds a low sombre note, and the proprietor raises his head.

His black hair looks spongy and moist as lichen. His whiskers bristle on either side of his long pointed face. He's sitting behind a scratched desk bearing an ancient cash register and a book catalogue, the corners of whose pages have turned up like dead leaves. His wrinkled eyelids rise lethargically as he stares at Mottershead, who strides forward and sticks out his hand. "Simon Mottershead. *Simon,*" he emphasizes to ensure there's no mistake.

The man gives the hand a discouraging glance and seems to brace himself as though his instinct is to recoil from his visitor. "Whom do you represent?"

"Myself," Mottershead says with a laugh which is meant to be self-deprecating but which comes out sounding wild. "I'm the writer."

"Which writer?"

"Simon Mottershead."

"Congratulations," the bookseller says with a distinct lack of enthusiasm. "To what do I owe such an honor?"

"I was wondering which of my books you might have."

"I can hardly tell you that if they haven't been published."

"They have been," Mottershead wails, struggling to recall titles which will help him fend off the blackness that seems about to consume him; he feels as if he no longer exists. *"Cadenza.* Even if it's out of print, you must have heard of that one."

"No must about it, I fear."

The shop is much longer than was apparent from outside: so long that its depths are almost lightless. The growing darkness might be the absence of his books made visible. "Let me tell you the story," he pleads, "and perhaps it'll come back to you."

The bookseller stands up and gazes past him. "You'll have to excuse me. I've a customer."

A moment later the bell tolls. Should Mottershead take advantage of the diversion and search the shelves for his name? Finding it in the face of the bookseller's denials would be the greatest triumph he can imagine. He edges past the desk and glances at the newcomer, and darkness rushes at him. "He isn't a customer," he says in a throttled voice.

"If he's about to make the same approach to me," the bookseller says, "I must ask you both to leave."

"Of course he isn't," Mottershead manages to articulate, rather than lay hands on his pursuer. "How could he?"

The bookseller opens a drawer of the desk and reaches into it. "Please leave or I'll have you excluded."

"You already have," Mottershead says bitterly, and lurches towards the exit, away from the tunnel of blackness which the shop feels like. The bald man is in his way. The top of his scalp is concave now, dented by his recent fall; his eyes have grown luridly bright, perhaps as a result of pressure on his brain. "You're a witness," Mottershead appeals to the bookseller, whose hand is still in the drawer, gripping a weapon or a telephone. "I've told this creature to stay away from me, otherwise I won't be responsible for my actions."

The bookseller shakes his head. "Please fight outside."

Mottershead sees himself and his tormentor as the bookseller is seeing them: two unpublished and probably unpublishable writers, mutually jealous because of their lack of success. The unfairness appalls him, and he's about to make a last attempt to persuade the bookseller of his authenticity when the bald man distracts him. "I've got something of yours," he says with a secretive grin.

"Whatever it is, you're welcome to it. Keep it as your fee for leaving me alone," Mottershead tells him, thinking that it must be the damaged copy of *Cadenza*. Since the other doesn't move, Mottershead lunges at him, and is gratified to see him flinch and cover his scalp with both hands. "Stay away or you'll get worse," Mottershead snarls, and marches out of the shop. Then his confidence deserts him, and he flees towards the open space beyond the avenue.

He won't stop for anything, he promises himself. The prospect of failing to find himself in yet another bookshop—of prolonging the black depression which seeps through him like poison—terrifies him, and yet he's unable to refrain from scanning the shopfronts in search of one more bookshop, one more excuse to hope. Didn't he behave like this when *Cadenza* was published? Was that the day when he flustered from bookshop to bookshop, feeling as though just one copy of the book would convince him he existed, until he was ready to do anything that would stop him feeling that way? He's dismayingly grateful that there seem to be no more bookshops on the avenue. Nevertheless a window causes him to falter: the window of a clothes shop.

He's past it—past the full-length mirror among the shirted torsos and bodiless legs dressed in kilts or trousers—before he knows what he has seen. He wavers, stumbles onwards, backtracks reluctantly. He sees himself reappear in the mirror, walking backwards like a figure in a video cassette playing in reverse. Under his suit, which is so faded that its pattern has vanished, he's wearing only a singlet full of ventilation holes through which the gray hairs of his chest sprout: neither a shirt nor socks.

So this is the image of himself which he has been presenting. No wonder everyone was leery of him. His reflection is beginning to tremble before his eyes; his helpless rage is shaking him. He's staring at the mirror as if he is hypnotizing himself—he's unable to look away from the sight of himself among the portions of bodies arranged like a work of art composed of dismemberment—when the man with the dented scalp appears behind him.

The reflection shivers like disturbed water. The movement seems to spread beyond the mirror, causing the torsos and severed limbs to stir as if they, or the single dusty head which lurks in one corner of the window, may be dreaming of recomposition. Perhaps one day he'll be able to derive a story from all this, Mottershead thinks desperately, but hasn't he already written something of the kind? His legs are pressing themselves together, his crossed hands are clutching his chest in an attempt to hide the discoloured flesh.

The other cranes over his shoulder, and Mottershead feels as if he has grown a second head. "Just a few words," the man whispers moistly in his ear.

"Suck a turd," Mottershead howls and staggers out of reach, bumping into the window as he twists around to face his pursuer. "Will those do? Will that satisfy you?"

The man rolls his eyes and licks his lips. Perhaps he's trying to adjust his teeth, but he looks as though he is asking for more. Mottershead shouts every insult and obscenity and combination of them he can think of, a monologue which seems endless and yet to need no breath. When at last he runs out of words, his victim hasn't even flinched. He raises one hand to his mouth to shove his teeth into place and gives Mottershead a disappointed look. "That didn't sound much like a writer."

"Then I can't be one, can I?" Mottershead says with a kind of hysterical triumph. "Happy now?"

The other reaches for his teeth again as a preamble to responding, but Mottershead won't hear another word. He knocks the hand aside and digging his fingers into the man's mouth, seizes the upper set of teeth. The tongue pokes bonelessly at his fingers but can't dislodge them until he has taken the teeth, which he shies across the avenue, narrowly missing a lone cyclist. "Fetch," he snarls.

His victim gapes at him as though the weight of his jowls is more than his jaw will sustain. Though he quails at the thought of encountering the tongue again, Mottershead plunges his fingers into the open mouth and grabs the lower set of teeth. Plucking them off the blackened gums, he throws them as high as he can.

They lodge in the branches of a chestnut, startling a bird, which flaps away along the avenue. "That should keep you busy for a while. Don't even dream of following," he warns, and runs after the bird.

Ahead, beyond a junction which puts an end to the shops, parkland stretches to the horizon. The sky above the park is cloudless, as though cleared by some emanation from the cropped grass. Here and there clumps of trees shade benches, all of which are unoccupied. As Mottershead passes the last shops the bird soars and seems to expand as it flaps blackly towards the zenith. Then it shrinks and vanishes before he expects it to do so, and he squeezes between two of the rusting cars which stand alongside the park.

The gates are held open by bolts driven deep into the path, cracking the concrete. Each of the stone gateposts is carved with a life-size figure which embraces the post and digs its face into the stone as though trying to hide or to see within. Above the scrawny limbs and torsos, the bald heads are pitted and overgrown with moss. Once he is through the gates Mottershead glances back, but the faces aren't emerging from the parkward sides of the posts, even if the moss on each of them resembles the beginnings of a face. Nor can he see anyone following him.

Beyond the gates the paths fan out. Most of them curve away between the benches, but one leads straight to the horizon, which is furred with trees. As Mottershead strolls along this path he seems to feel the city and everything which has befallen him withdrawing at least as far as the limits of the park. The grass is green as spring and sparkles with rain or dew, drops of which flash like windows to a microscopic world. He won't stop walking until he reaches the trees on the horizon, and perhaps not then unless he has grasped why the park is so familiar.

He's beyond the outermost of the benches when he begins to remember. He was walking with his family, his wife holding his hand and their son's, their daughter holding Mottershead's other hand. Shafts of misty sunlight through the foliage started the trees singing. He felt as if his family were guiding him, keeping him safe while his dreams took possession of the woods. He felt that he was being led towards the fulfillment of a dream he didn't know he had. Perhaps he was incapable of believing in it or even of conceiving it while he was awake.

In that case, how can he glimpse it now? Too many impressions are crowding it out of his head. Is it a memory, or could it be something he wrote or intended to write? Whichever, he feels certain that he recognizes the setting—that he has walked with his family through the woods at the far side of the park. They had a house beyond those woods. Isn't it possible that his wife and children still live there? That would mean he has a chance to make it up to them.

He can't think what he needs to put right, but surely he'll remember when he comes face to face with them. Did he use them in a story in some way that distressed them? He begins to jog towards the woods and then, as the trees remain stubbornly distant, to run. He seems to have got nowhere when he stops dead, having heard a toothless voice call his name.

He whirls around, snarling. The sky overhead seems to shrink and blacken, the clumps of trees appear to stiffen, clenching their branches. He can see nobody except a woman dashing through the gateway, dragged by three obese poodles dyed pink and green and purple, each dog wearing a cap and bells. Then the voice calls again, its speech blurred by the lack of teeth. "Here you are."

His tormentor must be hiding among the nearest clump of trees; Mottershead's rucksack is lolling on the bench they shade. He would happily abandon it, but if he doesn't confront his pursuer he's liable to be followed all the way to his family's house. He stalks towards the bench.

The man isn't in the trees around it. Mottershead can only assume the sight of the rucksack attracted his attention to the wrong clump. He grabs the rucksack and wriggles his arms into the straps, feeling a weight which must be the damaged copy of *Cadenza* settle on his back. "Thank you. Now please go away," he shouts.

The only movement is of the poodles, which are rolling on the grass near the gates so zealously that they've dragged their owner down with them. As Mottershead stares about, he notices that all the houses bordering the park sport television aerials. Was he on television? He seems to remember cameras being poked at him, lights blazing at him, technicians crowding around him. How many people saw him on their screens, and what did they see? Not knowing makes his surroundings feel like a concealed threat. "Stay away from my family, you lunatic," he cries, and runs back to the straight path.

He feels as if the contents of the rucksack are riding him, driving him towards the woods. Whenever he passes another clump of trees around a bench he scrutinizes them, though when he does so they appear to draw themselves up, to become identical with the previous clump. He's dizzy from peering around him and behind him by the time he reaches the end of the path.

Two trails lead from it into the woods. One is wide, and ribbed as though outlined by a giant ladder half buried in the earth. The other winds through a thicket, and he takes it at once, trusting the trees and the undergrowth to betray any attempt to pursue him.

The thicket is more extensive than he anticipates. The trees blot out the sky with branches so closely entangled that it's impossible to tell which foliage belongs to which. The leaves of the shrubs which mass between the trees, narrowing the path, look starved of sunlight; some are pale as the fungi which swell among the roots. Roots encroach on the gloomy path, so that he has to keep glancing down as he sidles through the thicket, peering ahead for the end.

At first he's able to ignore the way the darkness seems to creep closer around him whenever he examines the path, and then he tells himself that it's bound to grow darker as he progresses. But the darkness feels like a sign of pursuit—it feels like a sack which someone is poising over his head. Glaring over his shoulder, he sees that the thicket has closed in behind him, obscuring the view beyond it so thoroughly that the park and the city might never have been there at all.

Though he can neither see nor hear anyone pursuing him, his sense of being followed infests the woods. Foliage gathers overhead like eternal night, fungi goggle at him from beneath the mob of shrubs. He can't keep glancing back, because many of the shrubs between which the path meanders are full of thorns on which he's liable to tear himself. When he fixes his attention on the way ahead, however, he has the impression that he's allowing a pursuer to gain on him—that the dented head is about to crane over his shoulder, protruding its eyes and its discoloured tongue. "Stay out of my mind," he whispers, grabbing at branches and letting them whip savagely past him.

He feels as if he has ventured into a maze of thorns whose points are catching at his mind. He's tempted to retrace his tracks, but when he turns he sees that the branches which he let fly have blocked the path, rendering it indistinguishable in the gloom. At least the way ahead is passable, since initials and whole words are carved on the trees beside the path.

He's less inclined to welcome these signs of life once he succeeds in identifying the words. A tree to his left is inscribed vertically with one word: SOCKETS. A flap of bark has been left hanging from the next tree as though to expose the words DREAM OR SCREAM. Most disconcerting is the message displayed by a trunk on the opposite side of the path—NEARLY A TREE—because when he surveys the woods beyond it, several of the trees seem unconvincing, more like wood carved and assembled to masquerade as trees. He sidles between the thorns as rapidly as he dares in the gathering darkness.

The path bends sharply, and as he approaches the bend he observes that the trees directly ahead of him are carved with words from their roots to their crowns—tree after tree, leading his gaze into the depths of the woods. It seems to him that the thorny gloom must contain words enough to fill at least one book. Should he force his way through the bushes to read them? Perhaps the thorns won't injure him, for he's beginning to identify with them, beginning to think that the thorns themselves must have scratched the words on the trees; he can't imagine anyone struggling through the mass of them to do so. He feels as if the thorns aren't reaching for his mind after all, they're reaching out of it. He tries to grasp that impression, but it's too like an embodiment of the dark for comfort. He drags his gaze away from the engraved trees and edges along the path.

The woods are loath to release him. Thorns snag his rucksack and his shoulders; he feels as if the contents of the rucksack are trying to delay him. How long has he been stumbling through the woods? Will he ever be out of the dark? He's suppressing a fear that the path may have turned back on itself, because wherever he looks in order to pick his way he's confronted with paragraphs gouged out of timber. He's afraid to rest his gaze on them even for a moment, knowing that he'll be compelled to stand and read them while the darkness continues to gather.

Now the thorns ahead are rising above him, as though to drive him back. The rucksack tugs at his shoulders, the thorns overhead seem to writhe. He winces from side to side of the path, convinced that he can feel thorns reaching for his eyes. His left eye twinges as if the point of a thorn has touched the surface of the eyeball, and he claps one hand over his eyes and gropes forward with the other. The skin beneath his fingernails is tingling with apprehension. No thorns have pierced his fingertips, however, when the rucksack slumps against his spine and he flounders into the open.

It's almost as dark outside the forest as it was beneath the trees. Glancing back, he sees that he has emerged through a gap in a hedge which, in the darkness, looks impenetrable. The path, or his deviation from it, has led him into the back garden of a large two-storey house.

Light from a kitchen window and between the curtains of the adjacent ground-floor room lies on the worn grass, trapping him in the intervening darkness. He's preparing to dodge through the narrower ray and sneak around the building to the road when he recognizes the house. The curtains may not be familiar, but the gap-toothed look of the arch above the curtained window is, and the tilt of the bricked-up chimney and the droop of the handle of the back door. This was once his house.

The gap in the hedge was his doing. No wonder he was able to place the woods; they were his refuge whenever he found that he couldn't think in the house. He remembers taking care to leave the thorny branches intact, to make it harder for anyone to follow him. He remembers returning from the woods one day to find his children carving their initials on the kitchen doorpost, glancing fearfully towards him as the hedge creaked. His wife ran through the kitchen to rebuke them before he could lose his temper, but listening to her reasoning with them was more than he could bear. "Give me the knife," he said to her, and saw the blade flash in all their eyes. "Maybe one day people will know this was where we lived."

The initials are there on the jamb, all four sets of them. The pile of final letters appears to depict a steady hum, a lullaby which he can almost hear and which makes him feel dreamy and safe, home at last. The situation isn't so simple—he can't assume that he will be received with open arms—but surely once he sees his family he'll recall what happened in the interim. He creeps along the track of darkness, grinning in anticipation of the sight of their faces when they become aware of him. He's halfway across the lawn when a man appears beyond the gap between the curtains of the downstairs room.

Mottershead throws himself flat. The lawn feels like a mattress hardened by age, prickly and full of lumps. Is the man a burglar or some even more dangerous intruder? Mottershead gropes around himself in search of a weapon and finds a rake, its tines upturned a few inches in front of him. If he'd taken one more step before prostrating himself they would have had his eyes. He draws the rake towards him between the strips of light and begins to raise it through the shadow so as to grasp the handle.

The rake is perpendicular in front of him when he wonders if the man, who has passed the gap between the curtains, may be in the house by invitation. He can't assume that, he has to establish that his family is unharmed and not in danger. He has been pressing both hands on the tines of the rake in order to lift the handle; now he lets go with one in order to reach for it. His other hand can't support the weight, and the rake totters. As he tries to grab it with both hands, it falls into the light with a thump and a clang.

He digs his hands and face into the soil and lies absolutely still. The curtains rattle, the light spreads over him, and then the sash of the window bumps up. "Are you all right, old chap?" the man calls. "Stay there and we'll get you."

Mottershead seizes the rake and hauls himself to his feet. The man, who has a long face and a mane of reddish hair, looks concerned until he sees Mottershead clearly; then he frowns. "I lived here," Mottershead gabbles. "I'm just going."

"No hurry, old fellow. Perhaps you still do. Come round the front and we'll see if we can find your room. Shall we put the rake down? It's a bit late for gardening, don't you think? When it's light we can see about finding you your very own plot to look after."

Mottershead lets the rake drop. His embarrassment and discomfiture are giving way to panic, but he has to be certain that he's right to leave. "My wife and children aren't still here, are they?" he says as calmly as he can manage. "The Mottersheads."

"I'm sure they'll be here at visiting time. Let's go round the front now and I'll let you in."

Mottershead makes himself stroll to the corner of the house. As soon as it conceals him he breaks into a run, intending to be past the gates by the time the nurse opens the front door. But he slows to glance through the window in the side of the house.

Beyond the window is the dining-room. All the furniture has been replaced. About a dozen old folk wearing plastic bibs which cover their chests are seated at a trestle table draped with cellophane. Brawny nurses of both sexes stand behind them, spooning greenish slop into their toothless mouths or removing slices of bread which two of the diners have placed on their own heads. One nurse seems about to knock with her knuckles on a balding woman's skull but desists, simpering, when she catches sight of Mottershead. He puts on speed again, too tardily. As he rounds the house, the male nurse opens the front door.

He raises his long face towards Mottershead like a hound on the scent. "Sorry to have bothered you," Mottershead calls to him, backing towards the gates. "I should be somewhere else by now. I'll be on my way."

The man's face seems to elongate as his mouth opens. "We've someone who's a bit confused here. I don't think we want him wandering off."

He's addressing two of his colleagues, who have just stepped into the drive. Their eyes gleam with the light of the streetlamp outside the gates; the rest of their faces are covered with surgical masks. They move to either side of the drive and advance on Mottershead like mirror images, each stretching out a hand to take him by the arms.

He waits until they're almost upon him, his neck twitching as he watches them over his shoulder. At the last moment he dodges around them, leaping and nearly falling over what's left of his wife's rockery, and dashes across the car park which most of the front garden has become. He swings himself around an upright of a sign naming the Wild Rest Home and manages to drag the right-hand gate open as the concrete catches at its bolt. Struggling through the gap, he clashes the gate shut and looks back.

The nurses have already caught up with him. Though he didn't hear them following, all three are close enough to touch. The eyes of the masked nurses are far too large; their masks are so flat it seems impossible for them to be concealing any features. Their companion's face points like a hound's towards Mot-

tershead, and he poises himself, eager for the chase, as they each seize one of the gates. "Stay," Mottershead cries, and flees into the dark beyond the streetlamp.

Has he strayed back into the woods? Surely the suburban street ought to lead to a main road, but he's having to dodge around trees which sprout thickly from the pavement and even, it seems, from the roadway. There must be houses; he sees the flickering of televisions, though their screens appear to be among the trees themselves rather than in rooms. If he has turned the wrong way at the gates, it's too late to rectify his error. The single lamp has already been blotted out by trees dripping with mist, but he knows his pursuers are behind him. He runs towards the sound of an engine revving somewhere ahead.

It's a bus, and he doesn't care where it's going so long as it helps him escape. When he glances round he sees that the nurses are gaining on him, the long-faced man's nose quivering above the bared teeth, the others flanking him, their lack of faces glimmering. The sound of the engine is moving gradually to Mottershead's left, and he sprints in that direction, trying to avoid the patches of unsteady light where he glimpses figures watching televisions, unless the shapes are monumental statues which have collapsed in front of marble slabs. Then the long-faced nurse draws level with him, leaping over the source of one patch of flickering, which seems to freeze him for a moment so that Mottershead can see him clearly: face like a hound's skull, pallid flapping belly, limbs white and thin as bones. He drops to all fours and bounds ahead, ranging back and forth while he waits to see which way Mottershead will dodge.

233

Mottershead runs straight at him, praying that will make him falter. Instead the man leaps to meet him, his eyes bulging as whitely as his teeth. Mottershead lurches aside and puts on a final desperate burst of speed, which takes him away from the sound of the bus. There are no lights where he's running, only trees which loom in front of him whichever way he stumbles. "I won't go back," he tells himself, unable to say it aloud for the clamping of his jaw, feeling as though even his voice has deserted him. He swerves around another tree and another, and suddenly he's in a narrow passage where weeds and branches overhang the high walls. He dashes along it, tripping over bricks which have fallen from the walls, and at last it lets him into the open.

He's on a street which winds between dark dumpy houses. All the houses are derelict, as are the cars parked beneath smashed lamps along both sides of the road. Nevertheless the street isn't entirely lifeless; he hears the creaks of rusty springs, and several bunches of heads rise to watch him through the glassless windscreens, their tiny eyes glittering like raindrops. He peers along the brick passage, which for the moment is empty, and tries frantically to judge which way to run. The groaning of the engine becomes audible once more, and the bus grinds into view between the houses to his right.

The vehicle is dark except for its guttering headlamps. He stares at the passage again and sees three figures racing towards him, stretching out their arms until it seems they could finger the ground without stooping. He forces his way between two cars, and feels them shake as he disturbs their occupants. He staggers into the road, waving his hands wildly at the bus.

Is it really bound for somewhere called Frosty Biceps? He hasn't time to reread the destination, he's too busy trying to catch the attention of the driver, who is bent so low over the steering-wheel that his forehead appears to overhang his eyes. The driver sees him and lifts his expressionless face, whose features are squashed into a concavity between the jutting forehead and prominent chin. The vehicle slows, and Mottershead digs in his pocket for the envelope of money. The bus halts a few feet away from him and the door wavers open.

He hasn't reached the platform when the vehicle starts to trundle forward. Glancing behind him, he sees hands drumming their fingers on the walls at the end of the passage, three hands on each wall, as if his pursuers are only waiting for the bus to forsake him before they run him down. "Help me," he pleads.

The driver doesn't brake or look away from the road, but his forehead and chin relax sufficiently to let him open his mouth. "Get if you're getting," he mutters.

Mottershead clutches at the metal pole beyond the door and hauls himself onto the platform. At once the bus sways around the next curve, barely missing two derelict cars and almost throwing Mottershead off. He hangs on to the pole until the door drags shut like a curtain rusty with disuse, then he takes one hand from the pole to reach for the envelope. "Ferry?" he says hopefully.

"You'll end up where you have to go."

The driver seems to begrudge him even that response. Mottershead wraps his legs around the pole, feeling like a monkey, and tries to hold the envelope steady while he inserts a finger beneath the flap. "How much is it?"

The driver jerks his head, vaguely indicating the depths of the bus. "You'll have to deal with him."

Presumably he's referring to a conductor, but the vehicle is too dark for Mottershead to locate him. No doubt he'll come to Mottershead, who clambers upstairs as the bus sways onwards. As soon as he's on the top deck he clings to the banister above the stairs and peers through the grimy windows.

The passage down which he was chased is already out of sight, and the road is deserted. Otherwise the view behind him and ahead of him is less reassuring. The spaces between the houses are piled high with refuse: crumpled cars, bent supermarket trolleys, handless grandfather clocks hollow as coffins, huge verdigrised bells, television sets with doll-sized figures stuffed inside them, their faces and hands flattened against the cracked screens. He can't tell whether the hulks beyond the houses closest to the road are buildings or abandoned buses. He staggers to the front seat and falls into it, sitting forward to let the contents of the rucksack settle themselves, and then he sinks back.

There's movement above him. A round mirror is set in the ceiling over the cabin, allowing the driver to survey the top deck through a spyhole. Having spied Mottershead, the driver returns his attention to the windings of the road, and Mottershead looks back. As far as he can distinguish in the thick gloom, he's alone on the upper deck. He gazes ahead, willing the landing-stage not to be far.

He rather wishes he hadn't noticed the mirror. Its

bulbousness stretches the driver's forehead and chin so that his dwarfed eyes and nose and mouth appear to be set in a crescent of flesh surmounted by a tuft of whitish hair. The feeble headlights flicker over the derelict suburb, and Mottershead has the impression that the houses themselves are stuffed to their roofs with refuse; certainly the figures in the gaping windows are being thrust towards the sills by the tangled masses within. As the bus swings around a curve, scraping several cars, he thinks he sees a figure lose its hold on the second-floor sill where it's perched and fall head first onto the concrete. He can't be seeing all this, he tells himself; it's just that he hasn't had a chance to recover from the day, from the effect which the man with the unreal pate had on his mind. Another figure plummets from a window, the impact flinging its head and all its limbs in different directions, and he realizes that the figures are dummies. He shouldn't even be watching, he hasn't sorted out his fare. He tears open the envelope and brings it to his eyes.

It contains half a dozen coins and several folded notes. As he pulls out the notes and smooths them on his palm, the coins rattle together. Surely he has misheard the sound. He leafs through the notes, peering so hard at them that his vision shivers, then he glares at the coins. All of the latter are plastic, and apart from a note in some unrecognizably foreign currency, the notes are from a board game too.

He clenches his fists in helpless rage, crushing the notes, splintering the coins. So the writers' group never held a collection for him. The man who handed him the envelope must be responsible for its contents, and Mottershead is certain now that the man has been doing his best to drive him mad. When did he begin? He followed Mottershead into the room in the library, but from where? Perhaps from the bookshop where Mottershead found the copy of *Cadenza*—perhaps from the bedroom which Mottershead thought was a bookshop. The further back he tries to remember, the further and deeper the madness seems to reach; it's like a black pit into which he's falling with increasing speed. Then a glimpse of movement jerks him back into full awareness of his situation, and he glares at the mirror.

At first he thinks it may have been only the driver who moved. The man's face looks more misshapen than ever, the brow drawn further forward than the chin by the globular mirror. Beyond him, however, Mottershead can just discern the reflection of the lower deck, which is no longer empty. Some way down the aisle there's a hint of a face in the air, a glimmering of eyes and teeth.

The eyes and the grin must be dismayingly large to be visible at such a distance in the dark. They look deserted by flesh. He can see nothing of the head they occupy except for a pale scrawny blur, but he sees movement below them, in front of them. It has begun to reach two hands towards the stairs.

It's as though the mirror is a transparent egg inside which an embryo is forming. That image seems to clarify his vision, and he thinks the eyes are about to hatch or otherwise transform. Though neither the head nor the blur which is presumably its body has advanced, the thin white hands are much closer to the stairs. He can't tell whether the spindly arms or the hands themselves are lengthening, but he feels as if his seeing the shape is allowing it to reach out—as if his inability to look away or to stop seeing is attracting it to him. His fists close convulsively on useless paper and plastic. He shies everything he's holding at the mirror and scrabbles in his pockets. As the last of the notes flutters to the floor he finds the sharp portions of his broken credit card.

He takes them out and holds them between fingers and thumbs. There's one blade for each of his eyes. In the mirror the huge unblinking eyes above the knowing grin watch him. He lifts the points towards his face, trying to take aim despite the tremors which are spreading from his fingers to the rest of him. He'll have to apply the blades one at a time, he thinks. He tears his gaze away from the mirror, from the sight of the driver crouching over the wheel as if determined to ignore the presence in the aisle, the hands which appear to be drawing the rest of it towards the stairs. Mottershead grabs the back of his own head so that it can't flinch out of range, and poises the first blade in front of his left eye.

The bus has arrived at the brow of a hill, where the houses come to an end. Beyond the last ruins, whose walls are almost buried in refuse, the road snakes down a bare slope into blackness. At the foot of the hill is a looming mass relieved only by a few lit windows. His thinking is so constricted that at first he doesn't understand why the two lines of windows, one above the other, are identical. The lower rank is a reflection in black water; the windows are those of a boat.

Dare he risk heading for the stairs if that means the shape in the aisle may touch him? He'll never reach the ferry otherwise. The point wavers in front of his eye, his hand grasps the back of his skull. The bus accelerates downhill, and the sudden movement jerks his head towards the blade. With a choked scream he opens both hands just in time for it to scrape his cheekbone.

The plastic skates across the floor and clatters down the stairs. He still has a weapon, if such a defense will be any use. He mustn't imagine the worst or he'll be lost. The bus is more than halfway down the slope. He shoves himself off the seat and turns towards the stairs, bracing himself to confront what may be waiting at the bottom. But it isn't there, it's in the aisle behind him.

The rudimentary face grins with delight. The thin white fingers are visibly lengthening, and he has stumbled almost within their grasp. They're moving not so much like fingers as like the legs of spiders dangling in the gloom. If he hadn't stood up when he did they would have closed over his eyes. That thought and the sight of them paralyses him, but another swerve of the vehicle throws him forwards. A convulsion of panic sends him sideways, where he manages to duck away from them, onto the stairs. He's two steps down when they swoop over the banisters and touch him.

They touch his eyes. They feel like tongues composed of material softer than flesh. He hurls himself backwards, colliding with the metal wall, hacking at them with the blade. In the moment before they recoil from his attack he seems to feel a fingertip penetrating the surface of each eyeball. Blinking wildly, he slashes at the fingers as they retreat. Their substance tatters like wet paper, and he wonders if any of it is left in his eyes. As the remnants of the hands shrink back over the banister he staggers downstairs, moaning in his throat. "Stop," he screams.

If his plea has any effect on the driver, it causes him only to mime indifference. As he leans over the wheel, his features seem to retreat into the hollow between his forehead and chin. Mottershead lunges at the door and wrenches at the handle. Either as a result of his violence or because the driver has released the mechanism, the door folds inwards, but the vehicle maintains its speed. It swerves towards the landing-stage, which consists of no more than a few planks embedded in glistening mud. The bus is traveling so fast that it almost skids onto the planks. The driver brakes, and Mottershead seizes his chance. As the bus slows momentarily, he launches himself onto the stage.

His impetus carries him across the planks at a helpless run. They shift alarmingly, sliding sideways. Some of them aren't even set in the earth, they're floating in water which looks thick as mud. Before any of this has registered he's stumbling headlong onto the ferry as it bumps against the stage. By grabbing at the banister of the staircase which leads to the upper deck, he manages to halt himself. He clings to the rusty metal and stares back.

The bus is veering up the hill. Nothing appears to have followed him or to be about to follow. Though he can't hear or feel the working of the engine, the boat is drifting away from the stage, several dislodged planks of which are trailing in its wake. He feels hollow with relief, and so the boat is some way out before he notices that it has ceased to show any lights.

Could the crew have abandoned it while he was on the hill? Even being cast adrift seems preferable to his encounter on the bus. All the same, he would like to see where he's going. He scrambles upstairs to the top deck.

Several benches stand by the rail on either side of the deck. Ventilators rise above them, fat pipes whose wide mouths are turned towards the rail. Two pairs of double doors lead to a lounge below the wheelhouse. The sky and the water might be a single medium, a stagnant darkness which coats the surfaces of the vessel and fills the lounge and wheelhouse. He sits on a bench and watches the ruined suburb on the hill withdraw like a stage set and sink as though the blackness is consuming it, and then he sits and waits.

He isn't sure what he's waiting for: perhaps for daylight, or the appearance of another shore, or—best of all—of another boat with a crew to take him on board. He hopes he won't have to wait long, because it's beginning to prey on his nerves; he feels as if he isn't alone on the boat after all. The doors to the lounge keep stirring furtively as if someone is peeping between them. That could be due to the motion of the vessel, though its rocking is imperceptible, but what has he begun to glimpse in the mouths of the ventilators, ducking out of sight whenever he glares at them? Whatever is keeping him company, everything seems to conceal it; even the benches, which remind him increasingly of boxes with concealed lids. Perhaps the lids are about to shift. Certainly he senses movement close to him.

He grabs the rail and pulls himself to his feet. As he stares about the deck in the midst of the shoreless water he feels something dodge behind him. He presses his spine against the rail. The deck is deserted, but something is behind him. He's about to twist around until he catches sight of it, even though his instincts tell him that he won't succeed, that he'll go on spinning until he can't stop. Instead he makes himself stay as he is, and grips the rail to hold himself still. Before long he senses movement at his back.

He knows where it is. He might have known sooner, he thinks, if it hadn't been infecting his perceptions. He shoves himself away from the rail and strides to the middle of the deck, an expression which feels like a grin breaking out on his face. Planting his legs wide to steady himself, he shrugs off the rucksack and dumps it on the end of a bench. As he unbuckles it, the contents stir uneasily. He pulls it wide open and stoops to peer within.

There's no book inside. The only contents are a naked doll about two feet high. Though it's composed of whitish mottled plastic, it looks starved and withered. He inverts the rucksack, and the doll clatters in two pieces to the deck, the unscrewed top of the skull rolling away between the benches, the limbs twitching as the rest of the doll sprawls. What has emerged from the head scuttles into the depths of the rucksack and tries to burrow into a corner. Mottershead slams the rucksack onto the deck and stamps on it until the struggling inside it weakens and eventually ceases, then he kicks it and the doll overboard.

He hangs on to the rail and gazes at the water. Something is reluctant to let go of him. It feels like teeth buried in his brain, gnawing ratlike at its substance. As sluggish ripples spread through the water the teeth seem to burrow deeper and to lose their sharpness. The ripples fade as the doll and the rucksack sink, and he feels as if a toothless mouth has lodged in his skull, its enfeebled tongue poking at the fleshy petals of his brain. The ripples vanish, and so does the kiss in his brain, as if the mouth has been starved of brain matter. Now that his mind is clear he turns to see where the boat is approaching.

It's an island covered with trees and illuminated faintly by a crescent moon. Is it the place which feels as much like a dream as a memory? He has dreamed of being guided through the forest, following shafts of sunlight which appear to be both marking out his path and lingering on secrets of the forest: trees inscribed with messages of lichen; a glade encircled by mounds composed of moss and tiny blossoms as if the processes of growth are performing an arcane ritual; an avenue of pines whose trunks, which are straight as telephone poles, are surrounded by golden flakes of themselves as though sunlight has solidified in the piny chill and settled to the earth. Surely all this is more than a dream, despite his impression that the forest never ends—and then he sees that the ferry has brought him home.

The prow is pivoting towards the stage where he embarked before dawn. He can just see the avenue of poplars which leads to his house. Couldn't the forest which seems to cover most of the island be the source of his vision? There's no telling in the dark. At least the vessel isn't drifting aimlessly; someone is in the wheelhouse after all, steering the boat to the shore.

As the ferry nudges the stage Mottershead descends the stairs. Since there's nobody to moor the craft, he waits until the hull scrapes the tires at the edge of the stage, then he runs at the gap where the gangplank should be, and jumps. The ferry swings away at once and sails into the blackness, but he has time to glimpse the helmsman. Is it the bearded sailor from the earlier ferry? He's wearing a Balaclava, though he seems to have pulled it down over the whole of his face. If its dim silhouette represents the outline of the skull, then surely Mottershead ought to have noticed how odd the shape was. It's the fault of the darkness, he thinks, or else his perceptions aren't as undistorted as he has allowed himself to hope. He'll feel better once he's home. He turns away from the water and strides towards the house.

The poplars creak and sway as though they're about to collapse beneath the burden of the low thick sky. All the houses among the trees are unlit, and he can't locate any of them by the glow of the moon, within whose curve he seems to glimpse a hint of features. He feels as though he can sense the growth of the forest around him; he keeps his gaze fixed on the tarmac for fear of straying once again into the woods. When he sees the lights of his house ahead he sprints towards them.

It doesn't matter that he can't recall leaving the lights on. He runs up the overgrown path, fishing for his keys, which rattle out of his pocket like the chain of a miniature anchor. He's almost at the front door when he hears a voice beyond the curtains of the lounge: his own voice.

Worse yet, it sounds terrified. He feels as if he isn't really outside the house—as if only his terror is. He's tempted to flee into the woods rather than learn what the voice may have to tell him, but if he takes to his heels now he knows he will never be able to stop. He aims the key at the lock and grips his wrist with his other hand to steady it. At last the key finds the slot, and he eases the door open.

The bulb above the L-shaped hall is lit. The hall and the uncarpeted staircase look faded with disuse. Beyond the door to the lounge his voice is babbling incomprehensibly as if it's unable to stop. He retrieves his key and creeps into the hall, inching the door shut behind him.

He isn't stealthy enough. The voice is suddenly cut off, and he hears the whir of a speeding video tape. He slams the front door and racing across the hall, flings open the door to the lounge.

Three people are sitting in the slumped armchairs: a woman who may be about his age, a younger woman, a man her age or slightly older. All have graying hair, which seems premature in at least two of them, and faces so wide that their foreheads appear lower than they should. As Mottershead strides into the room the man jumps up and snatches a tape out of the video recorder while his sister clears away a board game strewn with plastic coins and toy notes. "Darling," the woman says to Mottershead, "we were just coming to fetch you."

"We've been wondering where you'd got to," says her daughter.

"Have you been working all this time, Dad?" the man says gently, as if Mottershead isn't already beset by enough questions of his own. Have they come to visit him, or are they living with him despite what he told the writers' group? Were they somewhere in the house when he left it, or did they let themselves in later? "I've been using my mind all right," he tells his son, to get rid of at least that question.

"Then I should put your feet up now," his wife advises.

"Take it easy," says his daughter. "You've earned the rest."

"Try and get some sleep," his son says. "We're here."

Why isn't Mottershead reassured? Part of him yearns to embrace them, and perhaps he'll be able to once he has watched the video cassette—once he no longer feels that they're keeping a secret from him. He knows they'll try to dissuade him from watching if they realize he means to do so. "Aren't we eating?" he suggests.

"If you're ready to put some flesh on yourself," says his wife.

"I'll help you," his daughter tells her, and they both go out. His son has slipped the video cassette into its case and is trying to pretend he isn't holding it. "I'll put that away," Mottershead informs him, staring hard at him until he hands over the cassette and trudges out of the room. "Close the door," Mottershead calls after him. "I'd like to be alone for a while."

The cassette has been recorded from a television broadcast. Handwritten on the label is the title, *Out of His Head*. Does that refer to the creative process? Might he just have heard himself reading one of his stories aloud? Again he seems to remember cameras and lights surrounding him, but now he has the disconcerting notion that it isn't the memory which is vague— it's rather that he was unsure at the time whether the crew and their equipment were actually present. He shoves the cassette into the expressionless black mouth of the player and turns the sound of the television low as the image shivers into focus.

The cassette hasn't been rewound completely; the program is under way. One of his books is hovering in space. *Postpone the Stone*—of course that was a title of his; why couldn't he have called it to mind when he needed to? A trick of the camera flips the book over like a playing card and transforms it into another of his novels, *Make No Bones,* and then into *Cadenza.* He's about to run the tape back to remind himself of his work when he hears what the commentary is saying about him.

"—speculate with an intensity best described as neurotic," an unctuous male voice is saying. "In one of his stories a man who's obsessed with the impossibility of knowing if he has died in his sleep convinces himself that he has, and is dreaming. Another concerns a man who believes he is being followed by a schizophrenic whose hallucinations are affecting his own perceptions, but the hallucinations prove to be the reality he has tried to avoid seeing. The reader is left suspecting that the schizophrenic is really a projection of the man himself."

Did Mottershead write that? He's reaching out to halt the tape, so as to have time to think, when he sees himself appear on the screen. The sight freezes him, his hands outstretched.

He's walking back and forth across a glade—whether in the forest on the island or behind his old home isn't clear—and muttering to himself as rapidly as he is walking. Now and then he lurches at trees to examine the bark or squats to scrutinize the grass, and then he's off again, muttering and scurrying. His grin is so fixed, and his eyes are so wide, that he looks afraid to do anything but grin. Every few seconds he digs his fingers into his unkempt scalp as if he feels it slipping.

While he has been straining unsuccessfully to distinguish his own words Mottershead has ceased to hear the commentary, but now he becomes conscious of it. "—in the last of his rare interviews," the voice is saying. "The price of such intense commitment to his work may have been an inability to stop. At first this took the form of a compulsion to tell his stories to anyone who could be persuaded to listen. Later, immediately prior to his breakdown, he appears to have been unable to grasp reality except as raw material to be shaped. The breakdown may have been precipitated by the creative urge continuing to make demands on him after he had lost the power to write."

He can almost remember telling stories to people in the street, to anyone who wasn't swift enough to elude him. He has the impression that the last such encounter may have been very recent indeed. Before he can seize the impression, his family enters the glade. They look younger, though their hair is already graying. They're trying to coax him home from the woods, but he keeps dodging them, both his gait and his voice speeding up. His babbling sounds more like the voice he overheard on his way in. He is still failing to understand its words when he hears his family murmuring outside the room.

He drags the cassette out of the player. He hasn't remembered everything; he's at the edge of a deeper blackness. He doesn't want to face his family until he has managed to remember. He hugs the cassette to his chest with both hands as if someone is about to take it from him. When the plastic carapace begins to crack, he's afraid that its contents may escape. He shoves the cassette into its case and stuffs the case into his pocket as he tiptoes to the door to hear what his family is murmuring about him. Before he reaches it, the voices cease.

He clasps the doorknob and presses his ear against a panel, but can hear nothing. He throws the door open, and the women turn to gaze at him from the kitchen at the far end of the hall, while his son comes to the doorway of the dining-room. "Anything we can do, Dad?" he says. "Want someone to sit with you?"

"I'm fine the way I am," Mottershead retorts, wondering how they can all have withdrawn so quickly from discussing him outside the lounge. He advances on his son, expecting to find that he has only been pretending to busy himself. But the table is laid; all four places on the dim tablecloth are set, except for one from which the steak knife is missing. He knows instinctively that it's his place. "You aren't finished," he stammers, and makes for the stairs.

The women continue to watch him. Under the fluorescent tube their hair looks gray with dust, their foreheads appear squashed by shadows. It seems to Mottershead that they may be about to transform, to reveal their true nature, of which these details are merely hints. His mind hasn't quite cleared itself, he thinks. He mustn't let this happen, not to them. "I'll be upstairs," he shouts. "No need to come looking."

"That's right, you put your feet up," his daughter
says.

"You've earned it," his son adds.

"Get some rest," says his wife.

Even this unnerves him; it revives an impression of
his life with them, of how it became a monotonous
descent by excruciatingly minute stages into a banality
with which he felt they were doing their best to
smother him. Or was that something he tried to write?
He dashes upstairs to his room.

He lies on the mattress and gazes at the branching
cracks and peeling plaster overhead. The sight makes
him uneasy, but so does the rest of the room: the
shapeless bulging contents of the chest of drawers, the
eternally open wardrobe, the blurred shapes in the
wallpaper, where he can see figures flattened like in-
sects if he lets himself. He closes his eyes, but shapes
gather behind the lids at once. Should he switch off the
light? He feels as if his sole means of finding peace
may be to retreat into the dark. He hasn't opened his
eyes when his family enters the room.

They must have come through the door from the
corridor. Even if he sees them standing on the side of
the room furthest from the door, they can't have
emerged from the wardrobe. "Having a snooze?" his
son says. "That's the ticket. We were just wondering if
you'd seen a knife."

"Why should I know where it is?"

"We aren't saying you do," his daughter assures
him. "You have your snooze while we see if it's anywhere."

He shouldn't have admitted that he knows what

they're searching for; he feels that the admission has made them wary of him. As they peer into the wardrobe and poke through the drawers full of unwashed clothes and fumble at the heavy curtains, he's sure that they are surreptitiously watching him. He inches his hands out on both sides of him and gropes under the mattress, but the knife isn't there. Suddenly afraid to find it, he shoves himself off the bed.

The three of them swing towards him as though they are affecting not to move. "We won't be long," his wife murmurs. "Just pretend we aren't here."

"Bathroom," Mottershead cries, thinking that he'll be alone in there if anywhere. He sprints along the corridor, past the rooms whose shaded light-bulbs steep the single beds in crimson, and into the bathroom, clawing at the bolt until it finds the socket. He crosses his wrists and clutches his shoulders as he stares around him.

The room is less of a refuge than he hoped, but at first he doesn't understand why. Is it the sound like a faint choked gurgling, not quite able to form words, which is making him reluctant to sit on the lid of the toilet or lie in the rusty bath? Though it can only be the plumbing, it seems like a memory, or at least reminiscent of one. His gaze roams the bathroom and is caught by a gleam beside the sink: his open razor.

If he's made to feel trapped in the room, he doesn't know what he might do. He scrabbles at the bolt, to get the door open before his family starts murmuring outside. The door bangs against the wall, and the heads crane out of the other rooms. His children appear flayed by the crimson light behind them, his wife's hair looks matted with dust; they seem to have hardly any foreheads. The sight appals him, and he flees past them, flinching out of reach. There's still somewhere he thinks he may be safe—the locked room.

The key was in the lock earlier, but suppose it has been removed while he was wandering? As he runs downstairs and along the corridor, he feels as though his nerves are all he is. He glances into the dining-room in case the knife has reappeared, but now the other knives are missing too. Even seeing the key in the locked door doesn't help; indeed, he wants to rush out of the house and never come back. But his hand is reaching with uncontrollable smoothness for the key. He turns it and pushes the door open, and switches on the light in the room.

A thought arrests him on the threshold of the bare room, which is so brightly lit by a shadeless bulb that it seems to contain nothing but illumination. Does he mean to lock the door in order to keep his family out, or himself in? Have they hidden the other knives from him? His vision begins to adjust, and he sees the walls white as blank pages, glaring like the walls of an inter-rogation room. Someone is lying on the floorboards under the bulb.

He can't immediately distinguish who it is, but he thinks that whoever has been persecuting him and his perceptions has managed to hide in the room. Since they are lying where the light is brightest, why can't he see them clearly? It occurs to him that he may not want to see. At once, before he has time to cover his eyes, he does. His family is in the room.

They're lying face up on the boards, their hands folded on their chests. His children's heads are nearest the door, his wife's feet are between them. At each of their throats a book lies open, pinned there by one of the knives driven deep. Their faces look as if someone has tried unsuccessfully to pull and knead and pummel them into a semblance of calm.

For a moment he believes they're watching him, though their eyes are dull with dust. But he's unable to waken any life in their eyes, even when he grabs the flex and moves the light-bulb back and forth, making their eyes gleam and go out, gleam and go out. Falling to his knees achieves nothing; all he can see is the book at his wife's throat. He finds himself reading and re-reading one sentence: "As a child he hoped life would never end; when he grew up he was afraid it might not."

He's rather proud of having phrased that. Did he once write about doing away with his family, or wasn't he able to write it? In either case, having already imagined the act and his ensuing grief may be the reason why he feels empty now, and growing emptier. He feels as if he's about to come to an end. Anything is preferable to the lifelessness of the room, even the kind of day he has been through.

He rises unsteadily and wavers to the door, where he switches off the light. That seems to help a little, and so does locking the door from the outside. "I'm better now," he mumbles, and then he shouts it through the house.

There's no response. He can't blame them for hiding from him while the fourth knife is at large, but if they'll only stay with him they'll be able to ensure that he doesn't find it first. He runs through the ground floor, hoping to meet them in each room, switching off the

light in each to remind him where he has already looked for them. He darkens the stairs and runs up, he turns off the lights in the bathroom, in his son's bedroom and his daughter's. Now only his and his wife's room remains, and mustn't he have had a reason to leave it until last? "Surprise," he cries, starting to laugh and weep as he throws the door open. But nobody is in the room.

He stares at the desertion, one hand on the lightswitch. Even the meager furniture seems hardly present. If he finds the knife he'll use it on himself. Why does the thought seem to contain a revelation? He clutches at his eyes with his free hand as if to adjust his vision, then he gazes ahead, barely seeing the room, not needing to see. He'll never find the knife, he realizes, because he has already turned it on himself.

Perhaps only he is dead. Perhaps everything else was a story which he has been telling to keep himself company in the dark or to convince himself that he still has some grasp of the world. He has to believe that of at least the contents of the locked room. No wonder his search for his family has shown him empty rooms; dreams can't be forced to appear. At least his instincts haven't failed him, since he has been darkening the house. He needs the dark so that his story can take shape.

He turns off the last light and pacing blindly to the bed, sinks onto the mattress. The room already seems less substantial. He lies back and crosses his hands on his chest, he closes his eyes and waits for them to fill with blank darkness. If he lies absolutely still, perhaps his family will come to him. Hasn't he tried this before, more than once, many times? Perhaps this time there will be light to lead them into the endless sunlit forest. It does no good to wish that he could return to a time when he might have been cured of his visions—when he was only mad.